"Blackwood's humor teases out the farcical aspect of human behavior at its most awkward and unmanageable, addressing outrageous situations with amused detachment and overtones of Gothic dread . . . She saw through pretense but knew that everyone wears a mask to survive an intolerable world, that everyone we encounter is engaged in a struggle we know nothing about. If we knew, we would probably die weeping. Blackwood felt it was better to die laughing."

—Gary Indiana

"Domesticity for Miss Blackwood has never been cozy; she listens for the ticking of the time bomb in the teapot."

—Carolyn Geiser, *New York Times Book Review*

"Caroline the pessimist made the world a happier place to be in because she could make mocking music of its terrors."

—Jonathan Raban

"The author writes with an appalled, amused intensity that is completely original but without a trace of pretentiousness. The result is unexpectedly powerful, like a box of chocolates with amphetamine centers."

—Francis Wyndham, *Sunday Times*

T0282140

"[Blackwood's] writing . . . is brilliant, black, like squid's ink squirted on the issues of the day, or, as in her best fiction, on relatives and friends who are thinly disguised recipients of her lacerating wit."

—Emma Tennant, *Burnt Diaries*

"She utilises black comedy as a means to engage with stories of the shocking difficulties faced by women and girls . . . Despite being a 'savagely original' voice and an irrepressible talent, Caroline Blackwood remains inexcusably neglected . . . Caroline Blackwood deserves to stand as a northern fiction author on par with her southern contemporary Edna O'Brien."

—Dawn Miranda Sherratt-Bado, *Irish Times*

"One of the greatest, darkest writers who ever lived . . . Her books are concise, mordant essays on evil . . . Blackwood's magnificent works are like pure odes to odium, her prose cuttingly matter-of-fact . . . Blackwood's works delve deeply into complicated, ugly relationships between women, something that is especially fascinating when the author herself was defined throughout her lifetime by her marriages to high-profile men."

—Virginia Feito, *CrimeReads*

THE STEPDAUGHTER

THE
STEPDAUGHTER

CAROLINE BLACKWOOD

WITH A FOREWORD BY HEIDI JULAVITS

McNally Editions

New York

McNally Editions
134 Prince St.
New York, NY 10012

ISBN: 978-1-96134-112-8
E-book: 978-1-961341-13-5

Design by Jonathan Lippincott

1   3   5   7   9   10   8   6   4   2

To Natalya, Genia, Ivana, Sheridan and Cal

FOREWORD

The other day, I went to the dentist on the Upper West Side. I've been going to this dentist for over ten years. I've been living in this city for over thirty-one years. Yet somehow, as I left the dentist's office, I found myself heading east on a block I'd never walked before. And while I was in the same neighborhood as a few sinisterly grand apartment buildings made famous by Hollywood—the Dakota (of *Rosemary's Baby*), the Ansonia (of *Single White Female*)—I'd never heard of, never mind stood in front of, a grand apartment building at 1 West 67th Street called the Hotel des Artistes.

The Hotel des Artistes was built in 1917 on what was once called "artists' row." Isadora Duncan lived at 1 East 67th Street. So did Norman Rockwell, Rudolph Valentino, and Noël Coward. In addition to double-height windows, the Hotel des Artistes had a squash court and a swimming pool. Meals were delivered to residents via dumbwaiter. The hotel wasn't catering to threadbare avant-garde types, but to commercially successful portrait painters, illustrators, and musicians who counted as their patrons New York's monied society families, many of whom lived nearby.

This building, in which a writer named Caroline Blackwood never lived, nonetheless calls to mind the spirit of Blackwood—born in Northern Ireland in 1931 to a Guinness mother and a multititled father, she attempted to escape the prissy drudgery of aristo-living for a more louche existence in London, attending "bohemian" parties that included guests like Princess Margaret—for the following reasons:

1. If a person had never read the work of Caroline Blackwood—which ranges from fiction to journalism—stumbling upon one of her books might feel like discovering a historic building in a well-trod neighborhood, and much self-condemnation might ensue. I personally condemned myself because before I read Caroline Blackwood's work, I "knew" her only through her minor character appearances in biographies of other people, where she was portrayed as the glamorous, well-bred, serial lover of famous men, and a source of good-copy gossip. It's genuinely squirmy to revisit the headlines of the reviews received by the 2002 biography of Blackwood, Nancy Schoenberger's *Dangerous Muse*, among them "Married to Greatness: Lady Caroline Blackwood Gained Fame Because of the Men She Seduced." Lucian Freud. Robert Lowell.

   Her fame-by-association identity was memorialized, or cemented, in the dramatic story of Lowell's death. Lowell had just left Blackwood in Ireland (his struggles with mental health and alcoholism strained the marriage, which was ending) and returned to New York. He was headed by cab to the home (at 15 West 67th Street, literally next door to the Hotel des Artistes) of his ex-wife, the writer Elizabeth Hardwick, while holding a painting of Blackwood by her ex-husband Lucian Freud, completed during *his* marriage to her, called *Girl in Bed*. Lowell, arms around a famous man's representation of his not-yet-ex-second-wife, died en route of a heart attack, his body discovered by his ex-first-wife when she was summoned outside by her doorman.

2. This story, or my memory of it, captures the heady, deliciously (from a biographer's perspective, at least) inbred world in which Blackwood lived, and the Hotel des Artistes represents, in building form, the hive-like intensity of artists, subjects, patrons, and money existing in close, intermixing proximity to one another. These people had sex with one another and painted one another and wrote about one another, yet their nonconformity was always padded, or glitzed, with the protective surround sound of money, power, status, and privilege. Which is not to say, contra Blackwood's Google bio shorthand ("writer and socialite"), that she was the dutiful gatekeeper of the milieu into which she was born; as a writer, she was its

beneficiary, true, but also its captive and its whistleblower. She revealed what was shadowy and malign behind and within the homes of the socially gilded. Often, in her books, strangers feature. These strangers invade the homes and manipulate or in other ways menace their ritzy inhabitants, puncturing their ways of life and, by means of destabilization, offering the possibility of escape. Blackwood might even qualify as a writer of psychological domestic horror. Her novels are the stories of people trapped by strangers, or by their own selves made newly strange inside beautiful homes.

3. Which returns me to Hotel des Artistes. The building, in fact, *was* featured in a Hollywood production: 1977's psychological horror movie *Audrey Rose*. A couple who lives in a beautiful apartment is visited by a stranger who tries to convince them that their daughter is the reincarnation of the daughter he lost in a car accident. Soon, the couple's daughter is calling the stranger "Daddy." It does not end well.

Blackwood is probably best known for two novels—*Great Granny Webster* (1977), an autobiographical story about a young girl forced to spend the summer with her aristocratic grandmother in a musty manse; and *Corrigan* (1984), about a housebound woman visited by a stranger who may or may not be after her money. These books feature *house as human condition*.

But it's Blackwood's nonfiction book *The Last of the Duchess* (1995) that offers the most interesting lens via which to view *The Stepdaughter*, her daringly cruel, knife blade of a novel, published in 1976. Both feature complex, often abusive acts of caretaking. *The Last of the Duchess* is about, in part, Blackwood's failed attempt to interview the aging, and infirm, Wallis Windsor. The duchess is either protected, or held captive, by her French lawyer, whose personal obsession with and tyrannical control over the duchess's legacy suggests the plot of a thriller. (Is Maître Blum poisoning the duchess with daily handfuls of "doctor-prescribed medication"? Will the duchess start hiding the pills beneath her tongue, then under her mattress, so that she can make a daring escape by throwing her body through a window, onto the roof of a passing Parisian garbage truck?) This question—protection or captivity—is never resolved, in part because the formulation is flawed. Caretaking, in *The Last of the Duchess* and in Blackwood's novel *The Stepdaughter*, is always defined as both. There's no choosing between them because the distinction does not exist.

The Stepdaughter, formatted as a series of unsent letters to "So and So," takes place in an apartment. A nice apartment, an apartment located in roughly the same neighborhood as Hotel des Artistes, with a similarly expansive view through the windows. The narrator, J, is the recently abandoned wife of a man, Arnold, who's disappeared to France with his new French lover. In their not-yet-divorce, he's ceded to her three belongings: the apartment; their four-year-old daughter, Sally Ann; and his thirteen-year-old stepdaughter, Renata. Also in the apartment: a French au pair named Monique. It's a mausoleum of luxury stuffed with women, all of them, save the au pair, victims (or beneficiaries) of neglect. Of the three younger characters, only Sally Ann is spared J's lacerating tendencies, if only because she is so rarely present or portrayed in the novel. J's self-loathing is so un-boundaried that any adjacent human becomes her target—which perhaps makes it an act of tremendously good mothering to keep the child beyond her field of perception.

The au pair, Monique, because her workload has suddenly increased and her freedom curtailed (she's rarely allowed out of the house), shows no more kindness toward J than she is meted out. She sees and judges (or is imagined, by J, to judge) J's near-total retreat from the emotional and logistical responsibilities of motherhood. "I am extremely upset today," J writes. "I have discovered that Monique loathes me. Yesterday I looked over her shoulder while she was scribbling one of her letters, and I read the phrase, '*la femme ici est abominable.*' I will never be able to forgive Monique for writing that apt and devastating sentence."

While Monique and Sally Ann are occasionally furloughed from the apartment, J and Renata, the stepdaughter, never leave. Their unceasing physical proximity renders Renata the most available collateral victim of J's self-contempt. J's initial treatment of her stepdaughter is so bracingly mocking and mean, Blackwood might be challenging the reader's first impression of J, baiting them to make quick assumptions, and to pigeonhole J as a bitter, bankrolled dilettante (she is a sometimes painter) with a spoiled child's tantrummy heart, in precisely the same way her husband, Arnold, might have done before he left her.

•

I NOTED EARLIER that *The Stepdaughter* is a cruel novel. I don't want to autobiographize Blackwood's work, but I experienced that cruelty—its complicated, gripping power and J's general state of despair and rage—as mapping back, however faintly, to Blackwood's own experiences as a woman whose identity, in a certain public's perception of her, was defined by the whims of other people's more notable lives.

There's no greater illustration of the self-determination headwind Blackwood faced than her entry in the index of *The Lives of Lucian Freud* (2020), a biography by William Feaver:

> Blackwood, Caroline
> LF's feelings for; marriage to LF; LF meets and courts; in Spain with LF; LF paints; Picasso makes advances to; and Barbara Skelton; Paris honeymoon and married life; health decline; revisits Paris; and LF's attitude to money; at Anne Fleming party; strained marriage relations; at Coombe Priory; in Arcachon; leaves LF; divorce from LF and marriage to Citkowitz; on LF's driving; "the Interview" (story)

Then there's this, from the text itself, announcing Blackwood's initial introduction to one of Freud's many lives: "Caroline Blackwood had been brought up to be eligible."

This might be, on Feaver's part, a perceptively sympathetic line. But given that it appears in the first of two cement-block volumes about a man who painted the

twenty-two-year-old Blackwood on their honeymoon—
"with [their] marriage came deflation," Feaver writes of
Freud, who, on this same honeymoon, vanished for two
days with a young girl, and who portrayed, in *Hotel Bed*,
his new wife as an emaciated, bedridden old woman—
that's not how I read it. Regardless, Feaver's quick slash of a
character summation/dismissal might give some indication
about where the rage of Blackwood's narrators, and this
includes *The Last of the Duchess* (where Blackwood is, in
fact, the narrator), might come from and why it manifests
as it does.

Because it often manifests as horrific cruelty and even
gothic disgust toward other women, and what might be
seen as their failure (or refusal) to be eligible, and how
that "failure" might be read as a form of critique to those
who've succeeded. In *The Last of the Duchess*, Blackwood
continually returns to what she sees as the grotesquery of
Maître Blum's aging body, in contrast to her surgically
altered face. ("Her face did not match her wizened little
hands which were those of a crone, and her age was also
betrayed by the discoloration of pigment, the brown flowers of death that discolored her arms.") She's also oddly fix-
ated with describing Maître Blum's appearance as Chinese,
her xenophobia deployed to offensively sketch Maître Blum
as a malevolent and powerful trickster. And, where men
are concerned: not eligible. Yet also formidable, wealthy,
and self-determined. Maître Blum, for all her wrathful,
vaudevillian energy—and her committed protection of
the duchess that seemed indistinguishable from elder
abuse—was a renowned lawyer whose clients included
Aga Khan and Rita Hayworth. She wrote crime novels

under a pseudonym. In Blackwood's portrayal (which, in later books about Maître Blum and the duchess, is echoed), she's a deranged, vain fantasist and prison warden; but for a woman, especially a French Jewish woman who became a successful lawyer in the early to middle twentieth century and survived the war, she's worthy of note, even respect. Blackwood's hysterically flamboyant portrayal starts to evolve, over time, into a surreal tribute to Maître Blum's unique, if possibly immoral or sociopathic, weirdness.

But buried in *The Last of the Duchess*, too, is a preoccupation, or acknowledgement of, multiple women viewed as accessories to famous people, and as such schemers. The Duchess. Maître Blum. And to some degree, Blackwood herself, accused of crassly achieving fame only through marrying the fame of others.

Seen through this depressingly familiar lens, J is a more domesticated version of a schemer. She's a jobless, freeloading '70s wife who lives comfortably and dabbles in painting. She might have once been eligible, but her eligibility has expired; her status has been rescinded by time, and she's been replaced with a younger version.

But what makes *The Stepdaughter* so compellingly radical—and ineligible—is how Blackwood unleashes a consuming female rage that cares nothing about protecting the innocent. J's candidly reported cruelty toward Renata, an actual child, who has been left in the care of a woman who hates her, creates a rule-defying atmosphere of emotional violence so potent as to reach beyond the borders of the page. About this child, J writes, "She had the pathos of those hopelessly flawed objects which one often sees being put up for sale in junk shops. She gave the immediate impression of having something vitally important missing." J also writes, "I found myself staring transfixed by the brightness of Renata's ugly orange shorts, which allowed one to see that her massive thighs were marked like an old woman's with little pocks of bluish fat." Much to J's disgust, Renata's only activity is making cakes from store-bought mixes. Renata bakes her cakes, and eats them, and then clogs the toilet with her huge, post-cake shits. She is the walking, if not talking (she's usually silent, and doesn't much interact with J) rejection of eligibility.

J's cool, logical, and perceptive understanding of herself contributes to the book's complicated addictiveness and allows the reader to continue reading without feeling as though they're a child abuse bystander or a sadist. J is acutely aware of the reasons she detests Renata, reasons that hairpin back to implicate or indict her. "I find Renata very ugly. I am therefore in no way jealous of her beauty, but in other ways my attitude towards her is much too horribly like the evil stepmother of Snow White. The girl obsesses me. All the anger I should feel for Arnold I feel for Renata."

Yet the real hero of the book *is* Renata. Like Maître Blum, she's the object of disgust *and* a source of slow-dawning admiration. J, who claims not to be jealous of Renata's beauty, comes to respect, even feel a bit chastened by, her self-sacrificing commitment to rejecting all that J represents. She consumes boxed, artificial sweetness through one hole and copiously empties it out through another, the foulness stopping up the plumbing that's hidden in the walls of the beautiful apartment. Despite Renata's withering portrayal by her stepmother, and despite her agonizing aloneness—no spoilers, so I'll only reveal that her mother has been committed to a mental hospital—Renata is the anti-J, being baked in this stifling oven of an apartment, fired by the heat of her stepmother's internalized misogyny, which her stepmother is, with every unsent sentence she writes, externalizing or exorcising by using, as her priest, this solitary, pre-woman child.

Which is not to idealize Renata's suffering. She is stunned by hopelessness; she is possibly self-destructive, even suicidal. Her failure to belong anywhere, to anyone, lends the novel a regularly breath-stealing sense of freefall. Eventually, the hermetic seal of the apartment is broken. People leave. Everyone, maybe, will survive, even thrive. But probably not. And while this book can be very difficult, at times, to read, I also found it impossible to stop reading. J, too, feels like a priest called to an exorcism. She shoves her own biases and hate—which are also the biases and hate of the culture, then and now—into the reader's face. The brief and unmediated confrontation with these durable demons is both chilling and exhilarating to brave.

Heidi Julavits
Berlin, 2024

THE STEPDAUGHTER

1

For weeks now I have been sitting in my apartment, which has a panoramic view of the splendours and squalors of Manhattan, and I have been writing letters in my head . . .

Dear So and So . . .

All day I have been staring out of my window at the jagged haphazard beauty of the city, with its dramatic amazing zig-zag of high and low buildings. I have been looking down at the great lanes of cars which look like psychotic insects as they try to race the sluggish Hudson. From my window I can see right across the river to the dirty brown smudge of buildings on the further shore, which seem to stretch to infinity in a never-ending urban sprawl. When Arnold and I lived in that dingy ground-floor apartment on West 82nd Street, I sometimes complained that I was someone who couldn't feel they were alive if they had to live in rooms which all looked out on to the same oppressive yellowy concrete wall. I told him that I had to have the illusion I was on top of things. Arnold is a clever man.

Like many clever men, he can sometimes be cruel. What can be crueler than to take someone at their word?

I am only writing letters in my head because I am jealous of the young French girl that Arnold has sent over to me from Paris. Monique is meant to help me take care of my apartment, my stepdaughter Renata, my own four-year-old daughter Sally Ann. She writes real letters whenever she is given a moment's peace to write them. My letters, which are written entirely out of rivalry, always end up as something unmailed and useless in my brain.

Sometimes I manage to take a sly glance over Monique's shoulder when she starts waiting, but I usually only decipher various names. 'Ma chère Maman'—'Mon cher Jean-Pierre'—'Ma chère Inez.' I am feverishly jealous whenever I see Monique getting out her airmail paper, because I know that whenever she starts scribbling with her ball-point pen, she has found, unlike me, a way to escape from my apartment. The girl is utterly wretched here. She looks as if she feels ready to die from home-sickness, loneliness and despair. When she came over to New York to learn English with a New York family, she could have hardly expected that the family would be like this. Although Monique has been working here for nearly two months, she can still hardly understand a word of English. This is not very surprising as very little English has recently been spoken in my apartment. I myself never address a word to Monique except when I have to give her instructions about the housework, which I mainly convey by miming with my hands. My stepdaughter never speaks to Monique either. But then Renata is like myself—for a long time she has not felt like speaking to anyone at all.

The lost, bored, frantic Monique is made to spend day after day listening to nothing but the incomprehensible four-year-old chatter of little Sally Ann. Monique is like a person who is being kept in solitary confinement in this apartment. When she tries to communicate with Sally Ann, it's with the desperation of some prisoner in an ancient dungeon who tries to save his sanity by talking to the rats.

Sally Ann very much dislikes Monique. The girl is incapable of understanding anything she says, and is therefore incapable of either controlling or amusing her. Lately Sally Ann seems to whine all day long. She is petulant, maddening and unmanageable. When she tries to come to me for attention, I shout for Monique and I make the girl take her off into a bedroom and shut the door.

Occasionally there are a few moments when Sally Ann is no particular trouble and starts to play by herself. At such times Monique immediately tries to write some letters, but I become jealous and I often manage to sabotage her attempt by insisting she take Sally Ann out to one of those sordid glass-strewn playgrounds in Central Park. The only times Monique has been allowed to get out of this overheated apartment have been when she has been forced to take the child out for some pointless, deadly walk.

Sometimes when I stare out at my view, it frightens me so much I want to pull down the blinds. I start to feel that all the owners of all the windows in the jagged sweep of the city's sky-line are starting to view the unforgivable way that I am treating this lonely foreign girl.

Every morning when I wake up, I decide that today is the day that I shall say something a little pleasant and friendly to Monique. My French is not bad. It is certainly good enough to make it possible for me to ask Monique a few dull, but kindly, questions. 'How do you like New York?'—'Do you find it very different from Paris?'

Every morning I promise myself that I will arrange for Monique to meet some French people, that I will take her to some New York bars and discotheques and parties, give her a chance to meet some kids of her own age. I find I never ask Monique any friendly questions. I never arrange to take her anywhere. The idea of going out on the town with Monique appalls me. She would be too gay and excited with her lovely toffee-brown arms. She would enjoy parties I could not enjoy—see a magic in people I am tired of. She would be asked to dance, and I can only imagine myself sitting alone watching her with the sour-eyed envy of some old-fashioned chaperone.

I find I have very little interest in trying to make Monique's American visit enjoyable. It is an effort for me even to give her a polite nod when I meet her in the mornings, seeing the way she not only writes real letters but also receives them. When the mail arrives I rush towards it as if I was expecting some important document. Always I get much the same pile of loathsome household bills. Monique gets hand-written airmail envelopes with French stamps. It is strange to realise that Arnold's letter from Paris, telling me that he wanted to leave me, is the last letter I shall ever receive from him. If he communicates with me in the future, he will do so through his lawyer. I have no wish to get a letter from Arnold. But often in the mornings I feel I would like to get a letter from someone. It is unhealthy the way I spend so much time alone shut up in my beautiful apartment. Sometimes I start to think that no one writes to me because I have been left by Arnold. I think the telephone rings much less than it used to before I was left by Arnold, When I become paranoid, I can start to feel such a pariah that I become very frightened of leaving my apartment. This would not matter if I could find something better to do in my apartment than behave unpleasantly to Monique . . .

Yours in all haste,

J.

Dearest . . .

I think about my treatment of Monique far too much. When I sit staring out at my view, I feel like asking the entire city of Manhattan why I am incapable of being a little nicer to this pleasant and helpful girl. Am I trying to punish her because, although she is temporarily trapped and suffering in my apartment, I know she will eventually work off the air-fare that Arnold paid for her to fly over from Paris—and she will escape? Do I hate her because she keeps reminding me that this apartment is my life—that it never need be hers?

Must stop. Will write again soon.

Yours ever,

J.

Dearest . . .

I am extremely upset today. I have discovered that Monique loathes me. Yesterday I looked over her shoulder while she was scribbling one of her letters, and I read the phrase, '*la femme ici est abominable*'. I will never be able to forgive Monique for writing that apt and devastating sentence. I feel tormented by the idea of that group of faceless French figures, Jean-Pierre, Jean-Claude, Inez, Marie-Claire, all of them eating escargots and drinking *vin ordinaire* far away in Paris, Toulon and Marseilles, and all of them seeing me just as Monique sees me, loathing me just as much as Monique loathes me. Their hatred haunts me as I look out at my view from a height that can sometimes give me the illusion I have been given control of New York City. If I could feel that Monique was unfair, I would like to write to every one of these French strangers and try to defend myself. But how would I ever persuade all these critical foreigners that there is not something utterly abominable about a tense New Yorker in her middle thirties who lolls around all day in her dressing gown, refusing to speak to either her daughter or her stepdaughter, while she stares out at her beautiful view and writes demented letters in her head?

In all haste as usual,

J.

Dear . . .

Why do I never write to a real friend, and yet keep complaining I never receive any real answers? Am I frightened to write real letters, because I know that if I was to describe my present state and my present behaviour to anyone who was fond of me, they would be so disgusted they would not want to reply? When I told you that recently I have often started to have the hideous feeling that all the inmates of all the buildings which comprise my view are reversing the process in order to view my treatment of Monique, I found it difficult to admit even to you that I also have an even more terrifying sensation. I feel convinced that they are all silently viewing my treatment of my stepdaughter. If I am being heartless, cold and exploitative in my dealings with Monique, I am being far more sadistic to Renata, who is only thirteen years old and is therefore far more vulnerable, for her whole life is within my control.

I find Renata very ugly. I am therefore in no way jealous of her beauty, but in other ways my attitude towards her is much too horribly like the evil stepmother of Snow White. The girl obsesses me. All the anger I should feel for Arnold I feel for Renata. If Arnold's letter from Paris was a shock to me—the thing that I found by far the most shocking about it was that he made absolutely no mention of any future plans to remove his hefty, damaged daughter from under my roof. Is Arnold going insane? Or is he being very cunning? Does Arnold really think that he can leave this fat neurotic girl in my apartment just as if she was some inanimate object like an umbrella that he happened to leave behind? Does Arnold with his calculating lawyer's mind really airily believe that if he is careful enough to make no mention of the girl, by some weird magic I shall somehow fail to notice the outrageous fact that she has been left with me? Does he want to try to let things drift in the hope that my customary inertia will prevent me from taking the necessary steps to get rid of her?

Sometimes, staring down at the lanes of congested traffic beside the Hudson, I make cruel decisions, in which I buy Renata an air ticket and quite simply despatch her, like a suitcase, to Arnold's Paris address. If Arnold imagines that he can start a new and beautiful life with his new and beautiful French girl, I can think of nothing more guaranteed to soil and smash his idyll than the arrival of this ungainly and unhappy girl who has survived the debris of her father's two former marriages. Sometimes I have even more vindictive fantasies in which I go to Renata and order her to pack her things. I tell her she no longer has any right to live in my apartment, and I push her out through the door, into the elevator, and out again on to the sidewalk as if she was some mangy cat I was letting loose on the city streets. In my imagination I then cable Arnold to tell him what I have done to his daughter and leave it up to him to act as he thinks fit.

Often I wake up shivering in the night and I start to wallow in my own self-disgust. If I thought that I could hurt Arnold, or merely inconvenience him, by acting out these unspeakable fantasies—can I be certain I would never carry them out? I would love to believe I am too warm-hearted, too decent, ever to try to take revenge on Arnold, by taking revenge on his child. So far I have been very restrained. My sadism has been entirely negative. If Renata is suffering from my treatment of her, she is suffering from things not done, rather than from any cruel things performed. Is this only because I know it to be a fact, that whatever abominable things I might do to his daughter—I could never make Arnold care?

Arnold has never seemed to be able to feel anything for Renata at all. He has never been able to pretend that her very existence was anything more than a monumental nuisance to him. He has always made it only too plain to me—only too plain to her—that if he could arrange it painlessly—for his own sake, as much as for her sake—Arnold would prefer Renata to be dead.

Two years ago, when Renata's mother became a chronic alcoholic with a tendency towards dangerous paranoid seizures and was placed in a mental institution in Los Angeles, Arnold was forced to take the custody of his eleven-year-old daughter. At the time he never pretended to me that he was in any way glad to do it. His curious middle-class conscience would not allow him to have his own child placed in a Los Angeles orphanage. Morally Arnold was trapped. Renata came to live with us because even Arnold's smart legal mind could think of no other suitable arrangement. Never did he attempt to make Renata feel that he wanted her. From the very beginning he made it quite plain that he felt deeply ashamed of her. I can still remember the expression of grim, raw embarrassment on Arnold's face when he first had to present her to me. Renata had just flown in from California, and Arnold had gone down to meet her at Kennedy Airport and had driven her back to our ground-floor apartment on West 82nd Street. Arnold, who is usually a man of immense social assurance, just stood there awkwardly with his daughter in the doorway, as if he had been struck so dumb he was incapable of introducing her to me. Arnold had not seen Renata since she was a small child, and the way she had developed was obviously profoundly shocking to him.

Renata was very tall for her age and so immensely overweight that the matronly spread of her huge body gave her the look of someone prematurely middle-aged. As the girl stood there miserably beside her father, who as usual was looking lean, elegant and well-dressed, I could hardly believe that Arnold was presenting me with his daughter. I kept thinking that she must really be one of his unmarried, unmarriageable aunts.

At that time I felt quite sorry for Renata as she stood there to be scrutinised and inspected by her strange new stepmother. She had the pathos of those hopelessly flawed objects which one often sees being put up for sale in junk shops. She gave the immediate impression of having something vitally important missing. She reminded me of some tea-pot with a missing spout, a compass that had lost its hands, an old-fashioned record that has had all its grooves badly scratched. She had a tense, half-apologetic, half-defiant expression on her face, which made one think that she herself felt that she had some kind of vital deficiency which made it unlikely that anyone could ever want her. The thing that Renata lacked so painfully was the very smallest grain of either physical or personal charm.

Everything about Renata I found instantly disturbing. She had poor thin hair which she had dyed a glaring peroxide yellow. She had lazily allowed the roots to grow out, and her skull was shocking in contrast, they were such an inky black. Her face was pudgy with lost, fat-buried features, and her skin was very bad, as if she had always lived on a diet of ice-cream and starch. She was wearing an orange and white T-shirt which had a really bold Californian bad taste. It emphasised the way that her bulging midriff was just as prominent as her bulging belly and breasts. I found myself staring transfixed by the brightness of Renata's ugly orange shorts, which allowed one to see that her massive thighs were marked like an old woman's with little pocks of bluish fat.

'I hope you will be very happy with us, Renata.' My voice had a brittle insincerity. I felt myself becoming ominously poised and slim and well-groomed while I looked at her. She made me feel far too feline. I had every advantage. I had the right to critically scrutinise her clothes, her general appearance and her manners. She was about to impose her presence on my household. I had all the strengths of my role. Even if I was magnanimous, I was still in the position of a martyr, while Renata was in the humiliating position of being an unwilling aggressor. Her humiliation was increased by the fact that her own father obviously felt immensely guilty that he was the criminal who was foisting her on to me.

Renata never answered when I gave her my brisk cool welcome. If I found this a little ungracious, I also felt that she was in some profound way correct. I kept wishing that Arnold could manage to hide his shame at having to present her to me. If he could only pretend that he thought she had some valuable, sympathetic qualities, I felt it might make it easier for me to accept the fact that this unappealing girl had come to live with me for forever. But Arnold has always been horrified by ugliness in young girls. He sees it as some violation of nature. It upsets him, as flowers upset him if he sees they have a blight on their petals. Arnold is also a man who likes women to do him credit. If he takes out a woman to a restaurant he likes her to have an electric effect on the other diners, so that they all crane their heads and stare at him with envy. Ever since Arnold had met Renata at Kennedy Airport, it must have been all too clear to him that there was no restaurant to which he could ever take his daughter where she was likely to make very much of a stir.

I could see from Arnold's irritated, baffled expression that he had found it quite impossible to make conversation to Renata on the drive with her back from the airport. In all fairness, I have to say that I can hardly blame Arnold for his failure. In the two years that I have now known her, I have never succeeded in sustaining more than a few seconds' trivial and superficial conversation with the girl. She is so frightened, so cramped, and so generally suspicious, she gives one the feeling that conversation is not something she in any way wants, and I'm afraid I've always felt only too happy to respect her desires. When I refuse to talk to Monique, it is not at all the same as my inability to talk to Renata. I would find it very easy to talk to Monique if I was not in a situation where I feel so ill-used that I have a churlish need to make everyone around me feel just as ill-used as I. I always found it quite impossible to make conversation to Renata, even when my frame of mind was much happier than it is now. I always had some kind of fear and dread of probing too deep into the workings of Renata's sad, sick mind. I never wanted to find out what Renata felt about anything. I preferred to see her as a lobotomised misfit, who was incapable of feeling anything very much at all.

'Would you like to see your room?' Arnold asked the girl. He made it so obvious that all he longed for was to get her out of his sight. He was already exhausted by trying to think up fatherly things to say to her. Renata nodded in that dumb, passive way she still nods if anyone asks her a question.

I showed the girl the bathroom, the closets she could use, the kitchen. I wondered if she was schizoid. She was like someone in a trance. I couldn't tell if she was taking anything in.

'You must be very tired after your flight. I expect you would like to go to your room and rest.'

Renata nodded with her usual irritating passivity.

After Renata had gone off into her room, Arnold poured himself a whisky.

'I guess that she will settle down.'

He didn't seem to feel like saying anything else about her, as if he thought that everything about Renata spoke for itself. When Arnold forced me to take Renata into my house as my second child, it was all too clear that Arnold felt that he had done something so terrible to me that it was beyond apology.

Arnold soon made an excuse to go out, and he stayed out very late into the night. From the very start I think he found it quite intolerable to have to watch Renata and me together. Our tense, unbending non-relationship seemed to arouse feelings of ill-ease and guilt in Arnold which he never learned to be able to face. Arnold had always chosen to remove himself from all painful human situations in order to pretend they do not exist. He seemed to travel much more after the girl arrived to live with us. He deliberately accepted work which took him out of New York. I think that when Arnold went out the night of Renata's arrival, in some deep sense he never really came back.

Although I find it humiliating to admit it, I think that Renata and myself soon started to blur in Arnold's mind, until we became virtually indistinguishable to him. He saw us as the same in the sense that we both made him feel that he had failed us. We muffled our grievances, but we both wanted him to be all the time aware of them. We paraded our scars.

In our very different ways Renata and myself managed to give Arnold the feeling that he would never be able to atone for the fearful injuries he had done us. He started to loathe being under the same roof as either of us. I very much fear that when Arnold put us both in this new apartment and left us forever, he got immense joy and satisfaction from his feeling that he was killing two oppressive birds with one stone.

In one perverse sense I have the idea that Arnold would have liked me to love Renata, even though he himself could hardly bring himself to look at her, that in some way he blamed and hated me because I was unable to do what he wanted. If I could have loved his daughter, Arnold would have had the emotional relief of knowing someone was doing his loving for him. He also wouldn't have had to feel any responsibility for the way I started to deteriorate in so many important ways after the girl arrived.

I had enjoyed looking after little Sally Ann until Renata came to live with me. Sally Ann was my first child, and I found her miraculous. I used to sit in the playgrounds in Central Park and feel relaxed and happy just to watch her dabbling with her pail in the sand pit. I felt amused and elated every time I made her laugh when I pushed her on the swings. At this moment I find it quite impossible to imagine how I ever got the very slightest pleasure from pushing Sally Ann on any swing. For far too long now I have felt that everything open and generous and affectionate in my nature has become sealed away from me. If I still retain any of these qualities, I can no longer get at them, for it's as if they have become locked up inside me in a safe made of grey steel with a complicated combination lock to which I have forgotten the key. I very much suspect that Sally Ann only whines so incessantly because she senses that my affection for her is no longer accessible—that if I was to watch her laughing on a swing at this moment I would not be able to see either her, or her swing, at all.

Very soon after Renata's arrival I found that Sally Ann was starting to exhaust me. In some complex way the presence of this uncouth stranger girl, to whom I was expected to become a mother, gave me such a feeling of inadequacy that I felt neither fitted nor inclined to play the role of a mother to anyone.

I made various token maternal gestures towards Renata. I got her into a private school. I saw that she was well fed. I tried to help her choose less ugly clothes. At the beginning I used to kiss Renata goodnight. When I look at her now I can't imagine how I ever managed to do it. But when she first arrived, although I never enjoyed it I made myself do it, and once it was done I would always secretly rub off the cold damp feeling her kiss had left on my cheek. I also used to read through all her abysmal school reports when they came in. Invariably they said that she was lacking in concentration, and co-ordination, that in all subjects she was inattentive and uncooperative and backward for her age, that she was totally incapable of being able to relate to her peers. I never showed them to Arnold. I knew it would bore and annoy him to have to

look at them. Renata's school reports still come in to me.
I doubt they show much improvement, but I will never
know, because I now throw them away without reading
them. Renata's scholastic progress is no longer anything
that interests me at all.

Even though from the beginning I arranged to see as
little of Renata as possible, considering we lived at such
unpleasantly close quarters, I was aware of her presence
all day long. I arranged for her to eat all her meals alone
in front of the TV set in her bedroom, but even when she
was in there watching some TV show with her door shut
I could never manage to forget she was in there. Although
superficially she was very little trouble to me—she troubled
me from morning to night. It is difficult to describe how
she manages to be so disturbing, this Humpty Dumpty of
a girl. She gives one the feeling that somewhere in the past
she took such a great fall that everything healthy in her personality was badly smashed. She seems to be crying out for
someone—let it be the King's Horses, let it be oneself—to
make some effort to put her together again. Too lazy, and
too selfish to wish to make this effort, one starts to loathe
her for imposing this unvoiced and unwelcome pressure.
By being so shy and vulnerable and giving out such a strong
feeling of being hopelessly damaged, she invites a kind of
cruelty. Renata's problems seem so insoluble that one starts
to feel such a fierce impatience with her that although I
hate to admit it one often has a longing to try to damage
her even more.

Although I always found it only too easy to understand
why Arnold wanted to have as little to do with Renata as
possible, I also perversely found that his attitude towards

her was heartless to a point at which I found it a little inhuman. I started to wonder whether anyone who was capable of behaving with such a freezing indifference to his own unfortunate child was capable of feeling anything very warm for anyone.

If Arnold found Renata repulsive, I felt it was his duty, as her father, to try to disguise it. I thought he was making it more difficult and unrewarding for me to take on the burden of this difficult girl, by allowing me to feel that he couldn't care less whether I was doing a good job or not. When Arnold came back from work in the evening, Renata would always be shut up watching the TV in her room. I can't remember one single occasion on which Arnold went in to see her. He never brought her any kind of gift, and he never once asked me how she was getting on in the household. I soon found that I could also never quite bring myself to mention Renata to Arnold. If Renata had superficially settled down, it seemed pointless and painful to try to complain to Arnold that it was myself who felt dangerously unsettled. I was becoming increasingly ill-tempered with little Sally Ann. I was sleeping very badly, and I never seemed to stop catching colds.

From nine until four Renata was away at school, but all day I found myself waiting in a state of irritable apprehension, dreading the moment when I would hear her key turning in the lock. 'Hi!' I would say as she came through the door. 'Hi!' she would answer cowering away, as if trying to avoid the blaze of hostility she knew she would see in my eyes. 'There's some raspberry mousse in the ice-box,' I would say. 'Oh great.' That would be the usual extent of our dialogue. After that, like someone trying to take refuge from a hail of bullets, Renata would quickly rush off and barricade herself in her room.

Must stop now. Have not too much more to say.

Yrs. ever

J.

Dearest . . .

Today is a Sunday. Sundays are always my worst days. Renata has no school. Since early morning she has been shut up watching TV in her room. I have never really known if Renata has ever particularly enjoyed watching TV I often wonder whether she can tell one programme from another. Sometimes I think she has only ever watched it in order to please me, that she has always been so frightened of the way I can only treat her with a crisp, false, kindly condescension, that she would be content to sit there watching the set just to appease me, even if it was not turned on. She is right to think I very much want her to watch it, because while she is tucked away out of sight, apparently engrossed in some stupid show, I can always pretend that Renata is happy, which relieves my constant, nagging feeling that I ought to be doing something to comfort the miserable child that must be lying somewhere behind Renata's graceless, displeasing facade.

I always think that I would dislike Renata's presence a little less if there was anything in the world that she liked doing. There is only one activity which has ever seemed to give her any positive pleasure, and unfortunately it has grated on my nerves from the very beginning, and lately it grates on them even more. Renata adores making instant cakes. If she would only make proper homemade cakes, using proper ingredients, butter, sugar, milk and flour, I might be able to respect it. But the cakes Renata makes require so little skill—they are ridiculously easy. She is far too old for me to find it very impressive when I see her putting on her baking apron. I have always felt infuriated by the way she is always so fatuously delighted by the shrivelled, rock-like objects she produces. I loathe the way she keeps opening the oven door in order to gaze at her cakes with the pride of the craftsman. Whenever she starts baking, I find she seems more than usually retarded, like a two-year-old making useless pies out of wet sand.

Renata's disgusting little cakes are the only thing in the world that she can make turn out a little as she wants. The only times I have ever seen her look slightly happy have been when she sees her cakes start to brown. I should find this sad. Instead I find it maddening. I hated to see her fat unhealthy figure baking in the kitchen of my last apartment. I hate to see her in the kitchen of my new one even more. More than ever in the last weeks, I have longed to get Renata out of my kitchen. I have always seen the kitchen as the heart of any household. I find it unbearable to have to share mine with Renata. Never has it seemed more important to me to have my kitchen to myself. For all I long for is to be allowed to sit alone in it, drinking black coffee, while I try to make up my mind what I am going to do with Arnold's daughter. All I long for is to be given a little privacy, so that I can try to clarify all my raging thoughts and feelings about my present situation by writing them out like incoherent letters in my head.

Yours ever,

J.

Dearest . . .

Yesterday Renata came out of her bedroom, and she made cakes all afternoon. Never once, since Renata has come to live with me, has she ever offered me one of her cakes when they are finished. As I have offered her so little, perhaps I should not be all that surprised by this. But always, when I watch Renata eating a whole plateful by herself, I find her unforgivably greedy and selfish. The moment Renata has finished eating one batch of cakes, she gets out more instant cake mixture and starts to make a new batch. Monique and Sally Ann are never offered any sample of Renata's cookery either. Renata has never paid the slightest attention to Sally Ann. She has never played with her, or even seemed really to notice her. The fact that Sally Ann is her half-sister has never seemed to mean anything to Renata. She treats the child with exactly the same indifference that Arnold has treated her.

Renata always makes the kitchen very messy when she cooks. She leaves all her dirty utensils to be washed by Monique. Renata never makes her own bed or tidies up her room. She treats Monique as her personal servant. She ignores her completely and takes it for granted that the girl is employed to do her chores. Although I myself can never bring myself to say a friendly word to Monique, I find that I loathe Renata for treating Monique with such an arrogant unfriendliness. I resent the way Renata never invites Monique in to her room to watch TV in the evenings. Renata and Monique are not very far apart in age. I feel that Renata should try to teach Monique a little English. Renata's weight is enormous, and I feel she should sometimes try to pull it. My apartment is on the top floor of a very expensive, well-built modern building. When I become fanciful, I find it very easy to imagine that Renata's weight is monumental enough to bring the whole apartment building down.

Yours ever,

J.

Dearest . . .

I am avoiding all my friends. When they telephone me and ask me out to dinner, I make excuses not to see them. I think about Renata so much that all my energies are dissipated and I feel unable to concentrate on anyone else. Within the first few days of Renata's arrival I noticed that she had a personal habit which I continue to find revolting. When Renata goes to the toilet she uses a crazy amount of paper, and she never bothers to flush the toilet. Renata seems to use up an entire toilet roll every time she goes to the bathroom, and when I come in after her I find the bowl of the toilet clogged with paper. On innumerable occasions when I have tried to flush the toilet after Renata has used it, the pipes have been so overburdened that they have regurgitated a swill of brown sewage all over the floor and I have been forced to call a plumber. I have never once complained to Renata, although I have always felt enraged when the plumber's bills come in to me. Maybe it would have been better for both of us if I had made a complaint, but something has always stopped me. I feel so hostile towards her that I have a horror of speaking of anything as intimate as her bathroom habits with this girl whom I still regard as a total stranger. More than ever at this moment I feel terrified of doing anything which might bring me

closer to Renata. If I was to make the wretched girl cry,
I am frightened that I might start to feel sorry for her,
and I want nothing to stop me from doing the one thing
I dream of. For I find I only manage to get through the
long days now by always dreaming of the moment when I
will send Renata back to Arnold and she will be once and
for all out of my life.

Yours ever,

J.

Dearest So and So,

Renata has really got to go! She has got to go very soon.
She is making me feel too petty. Today I found myself calculating the price of the toilet rolls I have to keep buying
from the supermarket, in order for Renata to waste them.
To punish her for what she costs me, I even found myself
planning to refuse to buy her any more packets of instant
cake-mix.

It is always possible that Renata's disgusting bathroom
habit is her way of trying to make her presence a little felt
in my apartment. If that has been her objective—she has
been only too successful. Whenever I go to the bathroom,
I most certainly feel that Renata has left her mark.

Yours hastily,

J.

Dearest . . .

When I sit in this beautiful apartment, I find it ironic
to think that I would not be here now if it had not been
for Renata. Our place on West 82nd Street was always too
small, but once Renata arrived it seemed to shrink so much

that I began to suffer from a constant sense of claustrophobia, as if I was being sandwiched between its floor and ceiling like a piece of ham between two wedges of bread. The kitchen there was much smaller than the kitchen of the apartment I occupy now. When Renata started baking, I found I could hardly get past the huge protruding behind of Renata when she was bending over the oven. I told Arnold I thought I would soon have a breakdown unless we employed a live-in maid. My whole life suddenly seemed to be only drudgery. I have always hated housework, and the housework seemed to have tripled since Renata arrived. I resented having to make the girl's bed, having to do her laundry, having to cook all her meals. Renata is completely helpless; she seems to have learnt to do nothing for herself. Her instant cake-making is the only form of cookery she knows how to do. She is frightened of kettles and is therefore incapable of even making herself a cup of coffee. She would be quite happy to live on nothing but her own cakes, but I found myself feeling so shocked by the unhealthiness of the diet she prefers that I always cooked her proper meals even though I did it with a very bad grace.

I told Arnold that I was suffering from headaches and anaemia, that I was over-fatigued to the point that the very slightest noise could make me jump. I could no longer bear to be forced to get up at six every morning to attend to Sally Ann. I was sick to death of the beds, the dusting, the dirty dishes, the child's incessant demands. I only wanted to go back to what I had done before I married. I only wanted to paint.

I blackmailed Arnold. I knew I was taking advantage of the fact that he felt in the wrong in having landed me with Renata. If I was being tough on Arnold, I really didn't care. I was determined to make him get me a better apartment. I was starting to resent him for travelling so much. Now when he accepted any work that took him out of New York, even if he was well paid for it, I still saw it as an abandonment. When he came back, he found me simmering with fury and discontent. I felt outraged that he had allowed me to spend so much time alone with Renata. I saw the girl as Arnold's personal burden, and I found it maddening that he should be free to fly around the world, while I was left at home to bear the brunt.

When Arnold went away I would find myself thinking more and more obsessively about the room which was occupied by Renata. It was the only room in the apartment where a live-in maid might have slept—the only room which I could have turned into a studio where I could paint. Renata's room could multiply in my mind to a point where I felt as angry as if she had taken away several rooms, all of which I would have liked to put to more rewarding use. I would find myself counting the days, and the years, that had to be got through until Renata would be old enough to leave home. I saw very little chance that she would ever be able to get into any college. I could never imagine her being able to hold even the most menial job. I could see little point in pinning my hopes on Renata's early marriage. But I would still try to cheer myself up by looking at all the photographs of ugly brides that were published in the papers. One has but one life to live, and even in my most optimistic moods I found it impossible to visualise the kind of man who would choose to spend that one precious life with Renata.

'You have changed,' Arnold told me. 'You are becoming a drag.'

Every word he said was true, but I still resented him for saying it. It was very easy for us to get baby-sitters. Arnold would have sometimes liked to go out to restaurants, and parties, and movies, as we had always done before Renata arrived. Now I always said that I felt far too tired and sick. I wanted to prevent Arnold from going out in the evenings. I also refused to invite any of our friends to dinner. I no longer wanted Arnold to enjoy himself. In the evenings I wanted Arnold to know what it was like to endure what I had to endure so much of the day. I wanted him to experience the deadening and depressing feeling that came from finding oneself cooped up in a small apartment with the silent, unhappy Renata.

Will continue when I find the time to write again.

Yrs,

J.

Dearest . . .

The expense of the maintenance of this new establishment terrified Arnold. It made him feel that I was pressuring him into overworking. Yet at the same time he never complained. He behaved very decently.

Arnold has behaved very decently to me ever since he decided to leave me. As a successful international lawyer, Arnold must know that he is under no legal obligation to treat me with the generosity that he has. He must know that he has the right to force me to move to a less expensive and viewless apartment. The separation agreement he has drawn up for me allots me far too large a share of his annual income. My own lawyer was baffled, quite openly disappointed. He would have preferred to have been able to fight for my rights—to have run me up astronomical legal fees.

Arnold is a very clever lawyer. When he wrote me from Paris and said that, although things had not worked out between us, his affection for me would never change— that he wanted above all things for me to feel financially secure—Arnold was merely being an affectionate, and clever lawyer. He no doubt worked out his letter with the same care with which he prepares his briefs. Often in legal documents the clause which is omitted from the contract can be more important than the ones put in. And the great clause omitted from Arnold's letter was the one that was there to warn me that I would continue to benefit from his excessive generosity only for as long as Renata remained in my custody and care.

Between every line of Arnold's tender farewell letter, in invisible ink was written his invisible blackmail. Arnold is very aware that we are still only at the first stage of the separation agreement. He would never dream of writing me any direct threat. He would find that unjudicial. He has still managed to convey to me his warning. If I refuse to continue to take responsibility for his disastrous daughter, my financial position in the ultimate terms of the divorce will most certainly be by no means as favourable as it is now.

At times I find it quite amazing that Arnold seems to be prepared to sacrifice such a large sum of money just to prevent his daughter from coming to live with him. At other times I don't find it amazing at all. If Renata can manage to irritate and upset me to a point that I feel quite unhinged by my disgust for my own lack of generosity towards her—the girl is bound to have a much deeper disruptive emotional effect upon Arnold. She comes from his ugly past—this ugly, untalented adolescent, whom no one wants, particularly her father. Renata does not come from my past. I see her as something even worse than my past: she is not only my present, she is also my future. That is why I find her presence in my apartment so intolerable.

Must stop now, as usual,

J.

Dearest . . .

All day I have been looking out at my view and I have been thinking about Renata's mother. I have been thinking about that woman with disgust and rage. Arnold always told me that she was a crazy, messed-up nymphomaniac, that he stayed with her for Renata's sake for as long as he could stand it, but when he felt she was really start-ing to destroy him—to save his life, he left. Sitting here alone, and going over Arnold's story in my head, I find it extremely difficult to believe it. I keep reminding myself that, as a lawyer, Arnold has been trained to do nothing except tell successful lies. In court, Arnold has always liked to defend men whom he has known were thieves and rap-ists. He has always far preferred to defend the guilty than the innocent, for he feels more pride in his own skill if he succeeds in getting them off.

If Arnold's wife was such a dangerously insane alco-holic, I find it very hard to understand why he took no legal steps to have the child removed from her care. He could always have placed Renata in a foster home if he felt incapable of looking after her. How could Arnold think that a woman who he felt was too dangerous for a grown man to live with would not endanger the life of a small girl? Arnold has been cold and unloving towards Renata recently, but he has not been irresponsible. Even I, who feel very critical of Arnold at this moment, find it hard to believe that he is a man who would be capable of walking off and leaving his own child in the charge of a woman who was out of her mind.

There is surely something very wrong with Arnold's story. As I stare out of my window I find that I often stop believing that Renata's mother is in a mental home in Los Angeles. I feel certain that she is really on the Caribbean on a yacht. I see her basking on the deck on a balmy, scented evening, and drinking iced-lemon daiquiris. As I see Renata's mother, her hair is drawn back by a white bandanna. She is wearing the scarlet top of a bathing suit, and her tanned midriff is bare. The elegant lines of her long legs show through the perfect fit of her snowy white summer slacks. She has very delicate wrists and they are braceleted with expensive jewellery. She is smoking as she lies back languidly in a canvas chair and enjoys the coolness of her drink.

I see a tall dark man standing behind Renata's mother. He looks Spanish or Italian. He is the kind of dark, handsome man I have never managed to attract. He is as perfectly dressed as she is, in a white tropical suit. He is quite obviously a millionaire and the owner of the yacht. As he fills up Renata's mother's glass, he whispers flirtatious compliments into her ear.

I feel enraged when I start to see this woman on her yacht. I see Renata's mother throwing back her head and laughing. I know only too well what she is amused by. She is laughing at me. She is only too delighted by the diabolical trick she has managed to play on me. For very obvious reasons this woman simply grew tired of the dreary and unrewarding day-to-day task of bringing up her unprepossessing daughter. She invented the whole story of her mental breakdown in Los Angeles. She cunningly foisted Renata on to Arnold, knowing that with his wily character he would very soon foist her off on to someone like me. Now Renata's mother feels she has a right to laugh, for she is a pleasure-loving woman and she is totally free to lead the glamorous and unhampered life she always needed to lead. She laughs because she knows that I often have to go out into the streets in the rain in order to buy myself a coffee from my local Schraffts, because I can't bear to go into my own kitchen because her daughter is in there making her infernal instant cakes.

I feel too upset and angry to continue.

Yrs. furiously,
J.

Dearest So and So . . .

There is something seriously the matter with me. When I start to shake with rage, feeling certain that I have been landed with the problematic Renata while her mother cruises the blue-green Caribbean waters, I know that something is going very wrong with my mind. I myself read some of the letters that Renata's mother wrote to Arnold from her mental institution in Los Angeles.

They were scrawled like a jerky temperature chart, and they had topsy-turvy writing all around the margins. She told Arnold about some visions she had had, which proved she had always been Florence Nightingale. She accused Arnold, and the other patients, and all the hospital attendants, of trying to dominate her brain waves. Her language was foul—horrible to see in print. All her letters were ugly and venomous, full of recriminations and threats. They were letters you wanted to burn the moment you read them, they were so obviously the hideous outpourings of a woman who was totally deranged.

In my cooler moments I know very well that Renata's mother is most certainly not romantically cruising, having craftily managed to dump her disastrous daughter in my life. As I write the words 'my life' I realise I mean my apartment. How it terrifies me to admit that I have allowed this apartment to become my only life.

Yours dismally,

J.

Dear . . .

Renata refuses to meet my eye when I speak to her. When I ask her what she wants me to order from the supermarket for her supper, her eyes dart furtively away from me, and she answers the ceiling and the wall. I know that this may simply be a nervous gesture because she feels frightened of me, but I still find myself wondering whether her extreme shiftiness of manner is not a sign that she is essentially dishonest. I can't stop myself thinking that all the faults of her father have been sown in the genes of this unfortunate fat girl. I seem to have been losing a lot of things lately—my comb, a bottle of hand lotion, my wrist watch, and my cigarette lighter. Every time I notice something missing, I feel instantly convinced that Renata has stolen it. Even when the missing items turn up (as they almost always do) I continue to blame Renata for having taken them, and I feel she only returned them out of guilt and panic. I find I can work up the idea that Renata is an incurable thief to such a point that I actually feel frightened to leave her alone in the apartment when I go out shopping, and at such moments I feel that I can never punish Arnold enough for having left me alone with a teenager so dangerously delinquent that she really belongs in some juvenile jail.

I feel that Arnold was extremely dishonest in the way that he left me: this may well be why I find it so easy to see the same dishonest traits in his daughter. All my friends tell me that Arnold wanted to marry his French girl for nearly a year before he let me know of her existence. Arnold's timing was excessively calculated, excessively crooked. He must have decided it would be unwise to upset me until I had been moved into my new apartment. I think that Arnold always hoped for too much from this apartment. It suited him to persuade himself that it would be such a solace to me, that I would be able to console myself with it as if it was a lover. He obviously hoped that my honeymoon with the apartment would have such a mellowing effect on me that I would feel no wish to contest his divorce.

I feel so humiliated now to realise that Arnold was over-feeding me like a fowl when he bought me this apartment. When he encouraged me to furnish it so expensively and promised to find me a French girl to help me with the children, Arnold was treating me like some wretched old bird which is fattened up just before the kill. One of the reasons why I feel so hostile to Monique is that I see her as one of the last specks of corn that was thrown to me by Arnold.

I can hardly bear to think that I once had the naive idea that Arnold was as excited as myself by the idea of our new and wonderful apartment. Arnold came with me when I went to real-estate agents. We both looked at the closet space, the heating systems, the general lay-out of innumerable unsatisfactory New York apartments, before we finally found the one that exactly suited our needs. Arnold had never before shown the very slightest interest in interior decoration. I was therefore very flattered and touched by the way he seemed so keen to help me look through paint catalogues in order to select the right colours for all the rooms. All my bitterness and resentment towards Arnold over the whole insoluble issue of Renata slowly started to vanish as he came with me to all the department stores and helped me choose pretty and exotic materials for all the chair and sofa covers—when he kept encouraging me to buy the most expensive furniture and rugs.

I am deeply ashamed to admit it now, but at that time I really believed that the sheer space and the luxury of the new apartment would solve all my problems. The new apartment had a bedroom for Sally Ann, a bedroom that would suit a live-in maid, and a bedroom for Renata. The bedroom for Arnold and myself was really spectacular, with many windows, which all looked out over a dazzling view. More important than all this, it had an extra pleasant well-lit room which I planned to turn into my studio where I could once again start to paint.

At that time I'm afraid that I really foolishly believed that all this precious new space would remove my depressive feeling that my life had become constricted, meaningless, without future. I thought I would be able to adjust to the unwelcome presence of Renata, as if I was no longer confined to an apartment where, even if the girl breathed in the night, I had the sense she was so much too close that her very breathing was giving me insomnia.

In the airy spaciousness of the new apartment I stupidly imagined that I would once again be able to feel young and gay and airy, that I would be able to feel that everything in my life was still capable of expanding, rather than condemned to a horrible prune-like shrinkage.

How ludicrous it seems now when I remember that I actually had the foolish fantasy that in our new and freshly-painted bedroom a new freshness would come back into my relationship with Arnold—that when we slept together it would be once again as it had been at the beginning, not like what it had become for us both in the last months, a mechanical and tiring activity, rather like doing push-ups in a gymnasium.

It is still very painful for me to realise, that all the time Arnold was helping me to move, he was all the time planning to leave me. When he helped me prepare the new apartment, he was preparing it as if he wanted it to be my last resting place. When he furnished it so expensively, he might just as well have been lining my coffin with velvet. But when Arnold laid me to rest in my last earthly abode, he made a mistake when he left me to rest there with a worm. Worms are meant to turn—but I am determined to turn on the worm. If I have to admit that I now have nothing in life except my apartment, I would surely be insane to allow my pleasure in it to be eaten away by the worm-like presence of that creepy girl Renata.

> Yours, determinedly,
>
> J.

Dear . . .

I am puzzled by my own irrational behaviour. Day after day I wander around my apartment in a state of suppressed fury, making life hellish for Monique and Sally Ann because I am so enraged that Arnold has left Renata with me. Yet I make no move to get rid of her. If her presence upsets me so much that I feel unable to settle down to start to paint until she has been sent away, what stops me from going to my lawyer and taking legal steps to have her removed? Arnold has got away with many things, but he can never force his abandoned wife to adopt the child of his former marriage. The most illiberal and woman-hating judge would surely have to take the view that Arnold was asking too much!

I would like to pretend that it was compassion for the appalling plight of this unwanted girl that makes me put off the day when I will finally shove her out through the door of my apartment. If I am honest, I would have to admit that there is nothing in the very least compassionate about my present behaviour. Nothing could be more unforgivably sadistic than the way I am allowing the unhappy girl to wait in a state of agonising suspense, never knowing what her father and I are planning to do with her.

Renata has obviously been intensely anxious lately. She senses that something has happened which is going to affect her life, and she lives in torment, never daring to ask me what it is. Her father has often been away before, but she must realise that he has never stayed away so long. In the past when he went abroad, he always telephoned at least every other day. Renata must notice that I never get a single letter or a call.

Recently she has been baking far more than her usual quota of instant cakes. Now, when she gobbles them down, it's as if she is hoping that in some camel-like way her body will be able to store them up and enable her to survive the desert future she fears must lie ahead.

She has also been leaving a really grotesque amount of unflushed paper in the toilet bowl whenever she uses the bathroom. In my silent way, I must have conveyed to her the fact that I am only living for the day when I can force her to join the unwilling Arnold.

Sometimes I wonder if she leaves so much paper in the toilet in order to rebuke me and remind me that since she has lived under my maternal care I have given her less human respect than I might give to a piece of unflushed toilet paper. Renata does not need to remind me. I know that I lack enough human respect for her even to have told her the truth about her horrible situation. I let the days slide by, and I stare out at my view, and I have still not managed to bring myself to break it to Renata that her father has gone off and left me—that the very last thing he wants is for her to join him—so that, although I can't abide the very sight of her, she has now really no one in the world but me.

Yours,

J.

Dear . . .

As the days go by, Renata is becoming increasingly miserable, anxious and unable to meet my eye. Her school has telephoned me several times to ask me if I know of any reason why she seems so exceptionally disturbed. It appears that several times in the last weeks she has suddenly burst into tears and run out of class for no apparent reason. The school feels that she is in urgent need of therapy Her work standards are dropping even lower than usual. I told her school principal that I would inform her father, who was abroad, that it was generally felt that Renata was in need of psychiatric help. I lied when I said that I had noticed nothing about her home behaviour that was in any way worrying or strange.

Lately I have noticed that Renata's eyes look permanently swollen, as if she spends her time crying when she is shut up alone in her room with the TV She seems to be getting fatter by the day. She is looking more and more puffy and unhealthy, because of her compulsive eating of instant cakes.

Monique looks almost as red-eyed as Renata, as if she too spends a lot of time crying whenever she is on her own. Monique looks much older and more careworn than when she first arrived to work for my family. She has given up taking any care with her appearance. She used to wash her lovely dark-brown hair every day when she first arrived from France. Understandably she no longer feels that there is any point, and her hair is hanging down in dark greasy strings. Renata and myself are still the only people that Monique knows in New York. She realises we are both in no mood to get much pleasure from the sight of her lovely freshly shampooed hair.

Monique finds Renata horrifying. She has no way of telling if all teenage New York girls are like that. Monique has a beautiful slim little figure. She seems appalled by the way that Renata slumps around the kitchen like a pregnant woman staggering under the burden of her own weight. Sometimes I see Monique looking at Renata with real terror as if she fears that at any moment this enormous girl might give birth to some kind of colossal messiah of an instant cake.

Renata's passion for her own specialised type of cookery disgusts, and completely mystifies, Monique. Monique is an excellent little classical cook and produces the most delicate and delicious meals. I ought to thank Monique. I ought to praise her. Instead I say nothing. I leave everything that Monique has prepared with great care and artistry untouched on my plate.

I am unhungry lately. After I have watched Renata consuming her own rock-like products, I feel that she has eaten enough for both of us. I am growing thin and scrawny. I blame Renata for making me lose my looks. I never want to marry again. But I still feel infuriated by the way that Arnold seems to be coldly planning to make me remain unmarried forever. Arnold would appear to have some kind of possessive double standard. He himself wants to re-marry, and he prefers to make me remain single so that he can always feel that I am alone and still waiting for him, if ever at some future date he might need me available. Arnold seems to be determined to try to make me keep his daughter. Arnold is an extremely worldly man. He must be only too well aware, that if I was ever to meet someone that I liked, my chances of marriage would hardly be likely to be improved at the moment when I would break it to my new beloved—that by gaining me, he would also be gaining Renata.

Yours in all bitterness,

J.

Dear . . .

Martha Weller is my best woman friend in New York, and I have offended her by making excuse after excuse not to see her. She has become militantly feminist lately, and I feel frightened of the harsh clear way she would appraise my situation. By trying to build me up a new confidence in myself as a woman, she might try to tear away what little shreds I still retain. To make me face the future, she would feel obliged to destroy my past, which is all at this moment that I feel I possess.

Martha would certainly point out that by allowing my whole personality and my career to be subordinated to the ego and ambitions of Arnold in order to benefit passively from the financial security he was able to provide me, my role in my marriage was little better than that of a prostitute. I was nothing more than a body bought by Arnold, and discarded when he found a prettier, younger one that pleased him better. Martha would dwell on the outcome of my life of failure until she would make it seem like an old-fashioned morality tale. She would not spare me the pain of being reminded that as the result of my own lack of responsibility to myself as a woman, I have ended up with most of my life over, with not a single accomplishment that I can take any pride in, except the acquisition of an excellent apartment and the permanent companionship of Renata.

Yours in great depression,

J.

Dear . . .

Even this excellent apartment has not been securely acquired. How can I ever bear the censorious and doctrinaire Martha to find out about that? It is certainly ironic to think that I only gained this apartment through Renata— and through Renata I shall lose it. I know very well that if I ever try to hoist Arnold with the petard of his own insoluble daughter, he will retaliate by legally refusing to maintain an establishment which he can rightfully claim is far too unnecessarily large and extravagant for one woman, with only one small child.

I hate to think that I have only been shilly-shallying in a state of frenzied indecision, tormenting Renata by keeping her dangling in suspense as to her future, because I am terrified of making the actual move that will lose me my apartment.

If I lose the apartment what do I fear I will lose? I have turned it into a human torture chamber. I would never have believed that I could have created such a little human hell from the very limited cast of characters who are within my control.

If I lose my apartment—I lose my beautiful view. But even my view is going sour on me. Yesterday, for once there was a little bit of pale wintry sun. I put on my fur coat and I went out to eat a picnic on my terrace. Sitting there looking out over the roof-tops, I seemed so far above all the noise, the smog and the poisonous exhaust fumes of the city that I could believe I was breathing fresh air. Then I looked down at the hard-boiled egg and the piece of bread-and-butter on my plate, and I noticed that in just a few minutes they had become mysteriously sprinkled with pepper. It disgusted me to realise that even up in the high clean atmosphere of my own sunny terrace my food was still being showered by the city's usual invisible rain of polluted soot.

At night lately, when I have looked out and my view has become magical and bejewelled, I have found myself envying all the people who live in all the rooms that lie behind the warm, gay, twinkling lights of the whole of Manhattan. I start to think they must all be leading warm, gay lives, in the rooms behind those lights—even in Harlem—even in Spanish Harlem . . . Surely this must be a sign that I am becoming a little insane.

Squalor, corruption, disease, cruelty, desperation, and violence—I can see no sign of these things, looking down from the height of my view. If they are anywhere they seem to be confined exclusively within the walls of my fine apartment.

At breakfast, when I read the newspapers, I find I now only choose to read accounts of disasters. I read about any victims of massacre or political torture—any victims of famine or earthquake. If there are any photographs of any dead, or burnt, or wounded, I study them with morbid interest. I like seeing pictures of bomb craters and devastated buildings. Anything interests me if it has received the full brutal force of military invasion and attack. I am happy to spend a very long time reading very long articles about the plight of the world's refugees, and sometimes I cut out the photographs of women with frozen faces, carrying the dangling bodies of their children. I find that I will now read anything that I think might make me feel lucky to be living here with Monique, and Sally Ann, and Renata, in the security of my splendid apartment.

Yours gloomily,

J.

Dear . . .

Yesterday the telephone kept ringing and I was afraid to answer it in case it was Martha Weller. I like her so much, and yet I feel I can't bear to see her. She sees me as an ill-used woman, and although I feel this to be only too true, my pride starts to resent it when Martha takes something that seems far too like some kind of vicarious pleasure in my plight. I also find it distasteful when not only Martha, but also Dodo and Rita and Alice, and the rest of my women friends, seem only to long to be allowed to rally around me like the crowds that collect around a street accident. I am afraid they all want the chance to champion my cause with much more ferocity than I feel able to face.

None of them ever liked Arnold, for he always found them plain and dissatisfied and argumentative, and he never bothered to try to use his charm on them. Now they all pine for a chance to fan my resentment at the way he has behaved to me. I hate the idea of seeing any of them, in case they find out the way that Arnold has made his one last public declaration of the deep contempt he must have always felt for me. By leaving Renata with me, he has shown his total confidence in my greed. He obviously feels insultingly secure in his belief that someone as parasitical and useless and greedy as myself would never give up Renata, if it meant that I would lose, not only her child support, but also my prestigious apartment.

If any of my women friends were to find out about Renata, I know only too well they would want me to hurl her back to Arnold as if she was a stone designed to strike his eyes out. They would be only too glad to paint Arnold as a fiend—and then they would advise me to throw Renata to the tender mercies of a fiend. In the interests of protecting my rights as a woman—they would not choose to see Renata as a woman. The complexity of their feminist ethics would confuse me. I am in such a confused state already, that I feel I cannot bear to hear anything that might make me further confused.

Yours distractedly,

J.

Dear . . .

All day I have sat around in a state of shivering tension in my apartment, as if I was imprisoned in some besieged and beleaguered out-post garrison, just praying for the relief forces I hoped might arrive with the dusk. What keeps me waiting as if I hoped some magical outside interference was going to save me from my intolerable situation? Surely I can't still be hoping that without any legal pressure from myself, Arnold will volunteer to take Renata to live with him, and I will thus be spared the unpleasantness of the wrangle that otherwise lies ahead.

Sometimes I think Arnold always knew that I would have great difficulty in taking any positive steps to get rid of the girl, that when put to the test I would be incapable of acting quite as ruthlessly as I would wish. Sitting here alone I curse Arnold for deliberately gambling on my kindness, or rather my weakness of heart.

Yesterday, when I had just made up my mind to make an appointment with my lawyer, I went into Renata's room when she was at school, and I found myself feeling intensely disturbed by the sight of her possessions. Except for the horrible Californian outfit in which she first appeared, she seems to own nothing that has not been bought for her by me. On her dressing table I saw the hairbrush I picked up for her at our local drug store, the string of wretched cheap beads that I gave her for her birthday. In her closet were the two pairs of jeans, the three T-shirts that I bought to be her school outfit. There was also the fancy nylon party dress that I got at Bloomingdales and told her was a present from Arnold. Otherwise she owns nothing except one orange lipstick, one pair of worn-out sneakers, and one pair of high-heeled shoes.

I found that I couldn't help wondering what Renata will go to—taking so little, when I force her out of my apartment. What will Arnold do with this ugly, speechless girl, even the very first night that she arrives at his Paris hotel? Will he take her out to dine at Maxim's with his French girl?

I assume that Arnold will almost instantly send Renata off to some boarding school—most likely to some French convent. As Arnold plans to live and work in France for a while, no doubt he will see that as the easiest, least time-consuming solution. I can never imagine Arnold ever bothering to take the trouble to find a school here in the United States which might suit Renata better. If Renata's scholastic difficulties are compounded by being suddenly plunged into a foreign system and language, I hardly think that Arnold and his girl are likely to care. I can only visualise Arnold's new French fiancée as being a ruthless self-centred and self-seeking bitch.

I find that I start to feel a completely illogical surge of fury when I think of the way she will treat Renata. I am convinced that she will encourage Arnold to feel there is no reason why he should take any emotional responsibility for Renata at all. If Arnold needs to be further poisoned against his daughter, his new French love will do that poisoning. I am certain that when she sees Renata she will refuse to have her in the house in the vacations. Renata will be packed off to some European holiday camp.

I keep trying to imagine how Renata will make out in a foreign, strange community—this uncouth girl who finds it so difficult to communicate even in her own language. All the time she has lived with me, I have never managed to make her say much more than 'Hi'—'O.K.'—'Right'—'That's great.' I can't help wondering if she will ever manage to learn the equivalents of those words in French.

Deprived of English-speaking TV programmes, how will that lonely frightened creature get through her days? At her new French convent it is most unlikely she will be given much opportunity to do any instant cake-making. Wrenched away from the few miserable little props which give her a grain of stability, if only from their familiarity, I can only assume Renata will deteriorate very fast—become increasingly recessive and maladjusted. Neither Arnold nor his new love will give a damn whether Renata has any chance to do her favourite baking. When I look at Renata's poor sparse possessions I feel only terror for her. I find it only too easy to imagine that she will end up permanently confined in a mental institution like her mother. Last night I had an even more ghastly vision, and it made me want to scream. I suddenly saw Renata, and she was dangling and blue-purple in the face. She was surrounded by French nuns, and they were all trying to cut her down. Her great body was limp, a horrible dead-weight as it dangled from the archway of the convent, where she had strung herself up with something that looked very simple, like the cord of her dressing gown.

Yours frantically,

J.

O dearest So and So,

I wish you were real enough to help me. I am becoming so irrational I am scared. I find it so easy to start seething with indignation when I think of the heartless way that Arnold's new fiancée is bound to treat Renata. And all the time I am furiously seething, Renata is shut up in her room in my apartment; and if the girl is crying, I am the last who will ever know it. Certainly nothing could induce me to go in and try to comfort Renata, knowing that I have nothing to say to her which could possibly cheer her up.

Dismally, as usual,

J.

Dearest . . .

Monique is leaving in two weeks' time. I had a sensation of total panic when she came to tell me that her working contract was so nearly over. It was almost as if I felt that my own time was running out.

By the time Monique goes, Renata must also go. My mind is made up. I have to put my own shaky mental stability in front of Renata's. I feel it could only be fatal for me to try to do what I could never bear to do. I know I would find it utterly intolerable to have to spend the next few years of my life cooking for that disorganised girl—scouring her baking pans, doing her washing and making her bed.

I have delayed the final moment of getting rid of Renata—partly out of a guilty terror of what will become of the helpless creature once she is sent off to France. But I am ashamed to admit that I have also been swayed by another, much more profound, terror. When Renata goes—what will become of myself?

I am only now starting to understand that all these miserable weeks I have been using that defenceless girl as my shield. By allowing my dilemma as to what should be done with Renata to consume my entire attention, I have felt entitled to postpone everything. She has made it possible for me to hide from my friends—to make not a single effort to rebuild my shattered life.

When Renata is gone, and I am no longer able to blame her for disrupting my concentration and my calm, I shall have to ask myself why I feel so little urge to paint. In my last apartment I could curse Renata for preventing me from working, by occupying the only room which I could have used as a studio. In this new apartment, my large light studio waits empty. I never enter it. My days have been wasted while I have sat brooding on the fate of Renata with an odious mixture of ferocity, pity and shame.

Recently I have hardly thought about Arnold except to loathe him for having left his daughter with me. Once his daughter has gone, I shall have to find out if my life can be richer, and better, without him. With Arnold gone, with Renata gone, I shall have to wonder if I am really a painter at all.

It may well turn out that my painting was only something that it was possible for me to do within the context of a marriage. While I was married to Arnold, I was able to regard my painting as a delightful creative hobby, that could be pursued on and off, without any particular intensity or professional seriousness. Since I was a child I have always had a little talent, but I have always lacked much drive to work to develop it. I have produced decorative canvases, rather I fear in the way that Victorian wives produced their water-colours, setting myself no standards, assuming that my husband and the world would think it clever and charming if I got out my palette and my easel at all.

Arnold never took my painting very seriously. 'Did you manage to get any painting done today?' he would ask. He might as well have been asking me if I had managed to get any household shopping done. Arnold thought it was good for me to have a hobby that I enjoyed, but when he moved me into this new apartment, it was certainly not to give me better facilities for working, it was to give me better facilities for taking on the responsibility of the upbringing of Renata.

Now, with Arnold gone, and Renata so nearly gone, I feel that my future career as a painter stands spot-lit and exposed. I am beginning to wonder if anyone is likely to see my painting as much more valuable than Renata's instant baking. It is starting to occur to me that, although I have much I can hold against Arnold, if he had pursued his legal career in the dilatory, dilettante way that I have pursued my own self-styled career, I should not now be sitting in this magnificent apartment, and the whole family would be on relief.

Yours despondently,

J.

Dearest . . .

I have decided that I humanly owe it to Renata to give her a little warning before I take legal procedures to have her shipped off to France. This morning I got up early in order to speak to her before she went off to school. She looked so grey-faced, so unhappy and exhausted, as if she had lain awake all night worrying, that I lost my nerve and decided it would be cruel to upset her just before she went off to her classes. Come what may, I shall speak to her this evening when she gets back from school.

Renata seemed a little more sympathetic than usual as I sat in the kitchen and watched her eating a plate of her own cakes for breakfast. This may only be because I have finally made up my mind to get her out of my life forever, and nothing ever seems so bad if one knows it is approaching its end.

Once Renata goes off to Arnold, I very much doubt that I shall have any more contact with her ever again. As we have formed no relationship in the years she has lived with me, there is nothing for us to keep up. I may never hear her name mentioned again once she goes out of the door of my apartment. It is most unlikely that Arnold will feel any need to write to keep me informed about Renata's progress and health.

Watching the girl eat her cakes, it struck me that I know as little about her past as I know about her future when she ceases to be my responsibility. I have no idea what she feels about her crazy violent mother. I have no idea how she feels about her rejecting unloving father. All I know is that something has made her move about in a very odd jerky way, as if she is always vainly trying to shed her ugly body in order to become invisible.

I could see that Renata hated the way I kept staring at her when she was eating her cakes, but she still seemed to feel forced to keep cramming them down her throat, as if she needed their nourishment to give her strength to bear my stare.

Looking at her, I wondered what it would be like to find oneself living in an apartment where one could not see one single good reason why one was living in it at all. With her father endlessly absent, the poor girl must often surely wonder what on earth she is doing here. It occurred to me that if Renata was in the hospital— if Renata was in prison—she would at least have the satisfaction of knowing the reason why she was there. That might be much better for Renata than being forced every day to wonder what she is doing in the apartment of a tense dark woman who gives a little start every time she comes in and finds her in her kitchen, as if she had just surprised a burglar who was making free with her food.

It also occurred to me that Renata may not be as upset as I imagine, when she hears she is being sent back to her father. If the girl is placed in Arnold's care, and he rejects and neglects her, as there is little doubt he will—at least she may be able to draw some emotional strength from knowing that she has every right to hate him. With me, even Renata's hatred has to be crippled, for she must know that she has very little right to resent me for my neglect, when neither by blood nor by temperament do I have any connection with her at all.

Although I keep trying to persuade myself that Renata will be quite glad to know she has to leave, all day I have felt extremely jittery, bad-tempered, and on edge. I have been swallowing fistfuls of Valium to try to calm myself, as I keep rehearsing the speech I am going to make to the girl. 'Renata, I don't know if you have guessed what has happened . . .' 'Renata, I am sure you won't be surprised by what I am going to tell you . . .' As I rehearse these speeches aloud, I notice that the tone of my own voice sounds most unpleasantly harsh and dry.

Yours apprehensively,

J.

2

Dearest . . .

This is the last time I shall ever write to you. I have written to you so often in these last wretched weeks, and if all my letters had not been imaginary I would now like to ask you to burn them. They all seem hectic and irrelevant. Everything is changed. Everything is over.

I see no point in writing to you any more, for I no longer have any need to clarify my own dilemma. Now I have no dilemma. I feel much calmer. At least I am no longer in the state of near-dementia which for me always seems to be produced by any state of agonising indecision. I have talked to Renata. Everything for me is over.

I went in to see Renata in her bedroom when she got back from school. She was sitting in an old wicker chair and watching a local news programme on the TV She never looked up when I came in.

'Renata,' I said in my carefully rehearsed voice. 'There is something I want to talk to you about.'

Renata went on staring at the TV I have been so enclosed in the last weeks, that I found it quite surprising to realise that there was still so much outside news—that it all seemed to be such bad news.

Renata was watching the most appalling fire which had just broken out in the Bronx. Glad to put off the moment when I would have to speak to her, I started watching it too. We both silently watched a house as it was stripped and gutted by flames. We watched the great, inky billows of smoke as they came belching from all its windows, and the firemen spluttered and choked as they battled to get their hoses near enough to souse the terrible blaze.

'How really ghastly,' I said. 'Do you know if anyone was hurt?'

'I expect they were,' Renata murmured. 'They haven't really said.'

The news programme went on to show an interview with a shifty pear-faced minor city official who had been accused of bribery and fiddling with the city funds.

'I wonder if you would mind turning off the TV for a moment. There is something quite important that I would like us both to discuss.'

Renata got up with an awkward flounce and pressed the button on the set so that the minor city official started to fade on the screen until his dishonest, protesting, pear-shaped face shrank to nothing more than a gleaming white dot.

'Why don't you come in the front room?' I said to Renata. Unless I sat on her bed there was nowhere for me to sit in Renata's room, and I found there was something distasteful about sitting on this weird girl's bed. 'It's so much more pleasant in the front room. Why don't we both go in there where it's really comfortable. It will be so much easier there for us to talk.'

Renata got up and followed me with what seemed like a very unwilling grace. I realised with a shock that Renata had hardly ever set foot in the front room before. The sight of my ominous hostile silhouette seated brooding on the window seat must have frightened her away.

The front room with its jungle of indoor plants, which were meant to give one the feeling of being close to nature— the front room blazing with the bold exotic colour of its Afghan rugs, which make such a calculated contrast to the white hessian cover for the sofa which after days of deliberation I had finally chosen with the help of Arnold—all the reproductions of Rouault, Matisse, and Klee, which, like Genet's *Notre Dame des Fleurs*, which lies open and unread on the coffee table, show this room to be the creation of a tasteful, modem sophisticate—all this was quite new to Renata, and she gave not a sign that she found it very impressive. Indeed, she looked so very much the opposite of comfortable when I seated her on the soft cushions of my sofa, that I realised she would have been very much happier if I had allowed her to have this upsetting conversation in the security of her own modest little room.

'I am sorry to have interrupted your TV, Renata, but there is something quite urgent that I feel I must talk to you about.'

She just sat there on the sofa looking extremely unhappy and frightened. I noticed she never once glanced at the room's vast plate windows. She had no interest at all in admiring my fantastic view.

'What do you want to speak to me about?'

'I don't know if you have realised it . . .' Despite all my rehearsals and my Valium, I found I was still starting to stutter, that I had none of my usual coolness and aplomb. 'I don't know if you have realised . . . that your father . . . that your father has decided to leave me.'

'I know that,' Renata said.

'How do you know that?'

'He told me that he was going to leave you.'

'Oh indeed! And when did Arnold tell you that, if I may ask?' A terrible, dry, sarcastic, brittle note was creeping into my voice—exactly the nasty note I had hoped to avoid in this whole conversation with Renata.

'He told me that he was going to leave you, just before he left for France.'

I examined Renata's face to see whether I could detect anything vengeful, malicious, or triumphant in her expression. I suddenly wondered how much she had always secretly hated me. Her pudgy face looked completely impassive. She gave not a sign that she realised what a cruel and shocking thing she had just said to me. She seemed unable to understand that I was bound to feel intensely outraged and humiliated by the fact that Arnold had felt a need to warn this frumpish girl that he was leaving—while he had felt no obligation to warn me.

'I really think that you might have said something to me, Renata. If you were told such a long time ago that my husband was planning to leave me—I think it was quite cruel and duplicitous the way you went on eating my food, and living in my house, and you never said a word to me.'

I wanted to accuse Renata, to blame her. I hoped to make her feel desperately upset and guilty. I was feeling a new kind of rage at the way Arnold had behaved to me, and some of the overflow of that fury was starting to spill out on to his daughter.

'I couldn't see there was any point in telling you,' Renata said. 'I knew that you would find out soon enough. As there was nothing I could do to stop him leaving you, I couldn't see what good telling you would do.'

It rather surprised me that Renata was capable of speaking to me in such a clear, flat, direct way.

'When Arnold chose to inform you of his imminent departure, did he give you any reasons why he was planning to leave me?'

'He said he found it hellish to stay with a woman once she started to loathe him for what he was—rather than for what he did. He said that he had found someone who loved him much more than you ever had. He said that he loved his new girl much more than he had ever been able to love you.'

Again Renata spoke with a total impassivity, as if she was only saying all this because she had been asked to do so. She seemed unable to grasp how unbearably painful it was for me to hear that Arnold had discussed me with her in this intimate way. It was shock enough for me to hear that Arnold had ever had any private conversations with Renata, when in public he seemed to feel no need to address her a single word.

'And when Arnold told you his reasons for breaking up our marriage—did he say anything about what he planned to do with you?'

'He said he thought it would be better if I stayed on here in this apartment.'

'Oh! Did he indeed!' I hoped Renata hadn't noticed the spiteful emphasis with which I said this. Now I had the perfect opening to deliver the sweet and sickly speech that I had been planning all day. 'You know I would really love for you to stay on here, Renata. I have been thinking about your future quite a lot. And though I know I am going to be very sorry to lose you—I have decided that it would be very wrong of me to allow you to be separated from your father. I shall miss you very much—but for your own sake I know that it's right that you should go to France to live with your father. I'm sure his new girlfriend will learn to love you, and that she will always be kind to you. You must remember that your father is your blood relation, and nothing can ever be the same as that.'

'Whatever happens to me—I can never live with Arnold!' The calm impassive expression on Renata's face had vanished. She suddenly seemed to be violently upset as if she was just about to cry. I flattered myself, for I thought she was trying to tell me that she only wanted to be allowed to stay on with me because I had always been so much kinder to her than her father.

'What makes you feel that you can never go to live with your father?' I hoped she would start to complain of the way he had always treated her. I wanted to hear nothing but bad things about Arnold. The fact that he had confided in Renata still festered.

'I can't ever live with him because he doesn't want me.'

'Why doesn't he want you?'

'He doesn't want me because I'm not his.'

'What do you mean—you are not his?'

'I'm just not his.'

'Whose are you then?'

'I don't know.' I would have found this grotesque conversation almost comic, if it had not come as such a devastating blow to me.

'How do you know that you aren't his?'

'He told me.'

'When did he tell you?'

'He told me when he was leaving mother. He said that he had just found out that I wasn't his—and that was the reason why he was leaving her.'

'I don't understand, Renata. Why did Arnold feel that he had to leave your mother because you weren't his?'

'He said that he would never have married her if he hadn't thought that I was his. When he found out mother had tricked him, he could never forgive her for making such a fool of him. He told me he loathed her so much—he never wanted to set eyes on her again.'

While Renata was talking, Sally Ann suddenly came rushing in to the front room and screaming. She was followed by a tense and flustered Monique. *'La petite s'est brulée!'*

Sally Ann's howls screeched in my ear drums. The sound seemed to be tearing larger holes in my already shattered nerves. The child kept trying to show me her hand. She tried to climb on to my lap, but I jumped up from the sofa and pushed her away.

'Pourquoi vous ne vous occupez pas de la petite?' I blazed at Monique. She went very red. *'La petite demande sa maman,'* she said accusingly.

'*Je suis en train de parler avec ma belle fille. C'est très important.* Can't you see? *Je ne veux absolument pas qu'on me dérange!*'

Sally Ann was still howling. She kept clutching at my waist as she tried to wind herself around me like a vine. 'What have you done to your hand?' I asked her irritably. Still sobbing, Sally Ann held it out to show me. She had very mild blisters on the tips of all her fingers.

'How did you do it?' I asked her.

'On the oven!' Sally Ann moaned. I learned later that Renata had left the oven on all night and it had been red hot when Sally Ann touched it.

'Monique will put it under the cold tap,' I said to her. 'I know it hurts—but there is nothing I can do about it. I'm afraid I can't be disturbed right now. I want to go on talking to Renata.'

Renata was sitting on the sofa as if she had gone into a trance. She seemed to have hardly noticed the whole commotion.

'For Christ's sake put the child's hand under the cold tap,' I snapped at Monique, hardly caring if she understood me. My French had failed me.

'Just get the child out of here! *Faîtes quelquechose pour l'amuser. Vous êtes ici pour vous occuper de l'enfant.* You are paid for that, Monique. I am in the middle of the most incredibly important conversation. I can't deal with Sally Ann at this moment. Don't you understand, Monique—I shall really go crazy if you let me be disturbed!'

'*La petite demande sa maman,*' Monique repeated sullenly.

'I don't care what she demands! I want her out of here. I want her out of here right this second!'

Monique hesitated, as if she was about to insult and defy me. She must have seen something so distraught and ferocious in my face that it made her frightened. She came sulkily over and picked up the unwilling Sally Ann and carried her off still screaming and kicking and writhing bodily out of the room.

'I'm very sorry about all that, Renata.' I suddenly felt an almost paranoid terror as I imagined the letters which would go off to France that evening. How inhumanly callous and odious my behaviour would seem to Inez and Marie-Claire when they received an account of my reaction to Sally Ann's little mishap, written in the merciless slanted handwriting of Monique.

'Please go on talking, Renata. I can't remember what it was that you were saying.'

'I was telling you that I wasn't his.'

'Oh, yes. I remember your telling me that only too well . . .'

'I have been planning to tell you for ages. I kept putting it off. I guess I was always too frightened. But now I'm very glad that you know.'

'It's certainly just as well to know these things, Renata.' My sarcasm seemed to frighten her, for she suddenly cringed away from me, as if she thought I was about to strike her in the face.

'There are still quite a lot of things I would like to know.' I now made an effort to make my voice sound more friendly. 'How did Arnold ever find all this out?'

'I got sick in Los Angeles,' Renata said. She spoke in an oddly detached way, as if she was describing something that had happened to someone else. 'I had to have a lot of blood tests. That was how Arnold found out what my blood group was. He told me the tests somehow proved that I had never really been his.'

'I think it was very cruel of Arnold to tell you all this,' I said. 'You must have felt ghastly when he told you about the tests, as if you were being accused and blamed for something that wasn't your fault. I think it was typically cruel of him to involve you in the whole thing. The whole business should have been kept a secret between Arnold and your mother. I think it was unforgivable of Arnold to feel such a need to drag you in.'

'I don't think it was cruel of him,' Renata said. 'I think it was very honest. Arnold said that he couldn't bear for me to think that he was a bad father to me. He felt it was much better for me to know the truth. He said that I would have to understand that as he had nothing to do with me he would never be able to love me. I think he wanted to stop me ever feeling hurt and disappointed about him.'

'And did Arnold manage to stop you feeling disappointed, Renata?'

'Oh yes, he did. For ages now I've known I shouldn't expect anything from him at all.'

We had a silence. I had the feeling that I was still incapable of fully taking in all the ramifications of the appalling thing that the girl had just told me. I got up to get a cigarette and it was almost as if I was drunk. I felt such a need to steady myself by holding on to the wall.

'I don't know if you understand, Renata, that everything you have just said has been the most tremendous shock to me!'

'I was afraid it would be a shock,' Renata said. 'I feel so bad about it. You have been so great to me.'

'I'm afraid I haven't been very great to you. I haven't been great to anyone lately. I haven't been great to myself. I've been in a very bad state lately. I don't know if you have realised what a ghastly state I have been in . . .'

'I know you have been in a very bad state ever since Arnold left, but I still think you have been great to me because you have never once got rough. I have seen you glaring at me as if you wanted to murder me and cut me up into little pieces—but you never once tried to hurt me. You never once got rough.'

'One can be quite rough on people, Renata,' I said awkwardly, 'without getting what you call rough.'

'I know that,' she said. 'That's why I have been trying to keep out of your way. Mother behaved just the same as you after Arnold left. She wouldn't go out of the house— she wouldn't eat. She just sat with tears in her eyes, sort of glaring out of the window. Mother wanted me to keep away from her—when she was in the same state as you . . .'

'What are you talking about, Renata? Whatever you may think about me, I really don't think you can claim that my behaviour has ever been at all like that of your mother.' I spoke much more sharply than I intended. In her naivety, Renata obviously couldn't understand that I found it extremely disagreeable to be told that my state of mind in any way resembled that of her deranged psychotic mother.

'Oh I know that mother got badly rough. But that was only at the end, when she took to the bottle and she really started to crack. But when Arnold first left her—she wasn't rough. She was just like you. I would try to be nice to her. But I could see she didn't want it. In the end I just gave up. I think she started to hate me because it was all my fault that Arnold had left her. You could tell she always loved him, and if she tricked him into marrying her, it was only because she couldn't think of any other way to get him. But Arnold wouldn't see it like that. He was shattered when he found out about the blood tests. He told me he had ruined his whole life for nothing and that now he felt the whole world was laughing at him.'

'What did your mother say when Arnold told her about the tests?'

'Mother admitted that I had never been Arnold's. She just couldn't understand why Arnold felt he could never forgive her. She didn't feel that she had done anything all that bad to him. Mother felt that, as it was, women had to do all the work for children—Arnold had no right to make such a big fuss about whether her child was his or not.'

'Did your mother ever tell you whose child you were, Renata?'

'No, she never told me. She didn't want to say I liked it better like that. I'd have hated for mother to have pointed out some slob of a guy working in some gasoline station. I'd have hated her to say, "Oh that's your father, Renata." It sounds crazy. But this way I like being able to choose the kind of father I would like to have. This way I can make him very good-looking and famous. Sometimes I think he's one of the big pop-singers—sometimes I think he's one of the racing car drivers that I see on TV I guess you will really think this is crazy. Sometimes I think I have got a father who is a king!'

'I don't think that is crazy, Renata. I find that very natural. There's still one thing I'm confused about—how do you feel about Arnold?'

'Oh, Arnold has always been really great to me.'

'I don't see why you think Arnold has been so great to you. He told you that he would never be able to love you. I can't see why you find that so wonderful.'

'Arnold was really great to me after mother got sick. He fixed it so that I could come here to live with both of you. If he didn't love me—if I wasn't his daughter—he didn't have to do that, did he?'

'He certainly didn't!' I wish I had not allowed such stridency and bitterness to creep into my voice. I felt exhausted. I wished that Renata would go back to her room. I only wanted to be left alone to think. I only wanted to be allowed to stare out at my view. But now Renata had made that impossible for me by telling me that her loathsome crazy mother had also liked to sit for days staring out of her window.

'Tell me a little bit more about your mother, Renata.'

'She was a very good person. She was very good till she got sick, and then she would start to have crazy rages. When she was in one of her rages, she didn't seem to quite know who she was. She would often throw things at me if I came into the room. But it wasn't as if she was throwing them at me. It was as if she didn't quite know who I was.'

'Did she ever throw things at your father—what I mean is, did she ever throw things at Arnold?'

'Did she throw things? Oh boy! He was often quite scared of her. She used to throw things at him, even before he found out about me. After that, of course, she got much worse, because he only wanted to call her names and accuse her. Mother always loved Arnold, but she kind of couldn't stop herself from throwing things at him. Mother was always so proud of Arnold—him being such a successful lawyer and all that. Mother's father kept a hot-dog stand in downtown Los Angeles. Mother wasn't used to money and the kind of swanky friends that Arnold had. Mother was a singer in one of the night clubs on the Strip when she was young. That's how Arnold met her. Mother was very pretty when she was young, but once Arnold married her and she had me, she got fat and she stopped being pretty. I think Arnold felt she gave him a raw deal. Mother would have loved Arnold to be proud of her—but he never was. He always made her feel he was very ashamed of her. He does that to me—but I'm kind of used to it. It made mother crazy. She always knew that she wasn't much good at things. Mother was a good cook. That was what she was best at. I'm crazy about cooking. I guess I get that from her . . .'

'I guess you do,' I said.

'Arnold says that mother is never going to get better,' Renata added. 'But I think that mother will. It was only the drinking that made her act so sick. I think that one of these days mother is going to decide she wants to quit all the drinking, and then she will come out of the hospital and be just like she used to be before she got herself into such a crazy mess.'

'I really hope so, Renata,' I said. 'But I don't think you should count on it too much.'

'I don't count on anything. I like to keep hoping, that's all.'

'It's been very nice talking to you, Renata. I hope you will excuse me, but I have some urgent letters which I really have to write. Why don't you go back to your TV Maybe later we can have another little talk about the future and decide what we both ought to do.'

I had the feeling that I couldn't bear to talk to her another second, to hear any more flat facts about her drab and painful life, even though she seemed much less freakish than she had ever seemed before to me, and I felt there had been great dignity in the cool, unemotional way she had tried to tell me about her gruesome past,

'You don't have to worry that I won't soon be leaving here,' she said, as soon as she got up to go. 'I have known for weeks that I couldn't stay on here.'

'What do you mean you will soon be leaving? Where on earth are you planning to go?'

'I'll soon be leaving. It's my problem where I go. Once I told you that I wasn't Arnold's, I always knew I could never stay on here. I can't bear to live in a place where I know I'm not wanted . . .'

'But of course you must stay on here, Renata,' I couldn't believe that I was actually saying it. 'Can't you understand, I really want you to go on living here . . . We will work things out. You may think it's crazy—but I'm quite glad to hear that you are not Arnold's daughter.'

I meant what I said. I was quite glad that, in any practical sense, Renata was now no one's. If I asked her to stay on with me, I could feel that I was doing it out of choice, and not because Arnold had crookedly pressured me into keeping her. All my old disgust and loathing for her was starting to disappear now that I no longer felt that all Arnold's faults were embedded in her poor clumsy frame. While Renata was talking about her horrendous life, I noticed for the first time that her face was only ugly because its features were distorted by fat. I found myself wondering if I could persuade her to go on a diet—if therapy could help her correct her unhealthy eating habits. Also, for the first time I noticed that she had very pretty eyes. They are the colour of the eyes of Siamese kittens, that deep greeny blue . . .

'There's only one thing that bothers me now, Renata. I feel hurt that Arnold never told me anything about your history when you first came to live with us.'

'But that was so great of Arnold. He knew you wouldn't want me in your house if you knew I wasn't his. When he was leaving for France, he advised me never to tell you. But once he had gone I felt I ought to be honest with you. I felt it was sneaky to go on living in your apartment without telling you the truth about myself. I know my mother would never have thought that was right . . .'

'O.K., O.K., Renata. For Christ's sake, let's forget it!' I knew I would never succeed in making the girl understand that Arnold's behaviour, which she saw as so great and wonderful, could only be seen as utterly corrupt and despicable by me.

'I'll be leaving soon. Don't you worry,' Renata said as she went off to her room. 'I couldn't ever feel comfortable living here now that you know I'm not what you thought.'

'Don't be such a little idiot, Renata!' I shouted. 'You are going to stay on here. I absolutely insist on it. I feel I am very lucky to have you . . .' I don't know if Renata heard, because she had already turned on the TV

Do you understand, dear So and So, why I said that everything was over? I am much calmer now, if only because I no longer feel plagued by any options. I shall keep Renata, and with a little luck our future together won't turn out to be all that much worse than futures usually have to be. I think we shall be able to bump along together without bruising each other unnecessarily. I have a feeling of optimism and bigness at the moment. I only hope I will be strong enough to sustain it. I only pray that I will never allow this new bigness to be punctured by any aggravating smallness—Renata's bathroom habits for example. Wish me luck, dear So and So. Wish both Renata and me a lot of luck.

Yours hopefully,
J.

Dearest So and So . . .

I said I was never going to write to you again. You only hear from me now because I am so worried I feel I am going out of my mind. Renata has disappeared. She vanished three nights ago. She must have crept out of the apartment only a few hours after we had both finished that painful discussion in which we dredged up some of the brutal facts about her past. I never heard Renata leave because I was sitting in the front room looking out at my view and thinking over all the things she had told me.

One of the many reasons why her disappearance makes me feel so ghastly is that I know that if I had only gone in to say goodnight to her in her bedroom it might never have happened.

I should have realised that she was bound to be in a state of great distress that evening. Our conversation obviously had to be an agonising ordeal for someone as raw and timid as Renata. In all the time I have known the girl she has probably never been in quite such urgent need of a little reassurance and affection as she was that night. But I just left her alone in her room, shut up with nothing but the torment of her own frightened thoughts and the TV Now that she has vanished, I wonder how I will ever be able to forgive myself.

The terrible truth is that I felt too tired to go in and see Renata in her bedroom that evening. In view of what has happened, my excuse that I was too exhausted has to seem a very feeble one. But I still have to say that my conversation with the girl has left me feeling indescribably fatigued. After we had finished our talk I just sat staring out of the window, feeling even too weak to take a few steps across the apartment to get to my own bed. In my whole life I have hardly ever felt quite so wrung-out, drained, and flattened, as if like some damp sheet I had just been passed through the crushing rollers of a mangle.

I know that it has to sound monstrously selfish now, but that evening I felt I really couldn't bear if it I had to speak to Renata any more. It seemed to me that we had both talked far too much that day already. Now I realise that I should have gone into her room and told her once again how much I wanted her to go on living with me.

But at the time I had a horror of having to say one more word to her. I felt I couldn't stand the very sight of her forlorn and apprehensive face until I had been allowed a little time to myself to recover from the impact of all the shattering things she had told me. I planned, of course, to be exceptionally nice to her in the morning.

It was Monique who first announced that Renata had gone, when she went to wake her up for school. The girl's bedroom was a horrible sight. Her bed had not been slept in, and there was something eerily deliberate in the way that she had stripped it completely bare, leaving not even a piece of crumpled Kleenex in the waste-paper basket or a speck of spilled face-powder on the dressing table to show any sign that she had ever occupied the room at all. It appeared that she had thrown her entire possessions into some old canvas bag. I found it extremely painful to be reminded all over again how very few things Renata had.

There was no evidence that she had taken a scrap of food from the kitchen, not even a cheese cracker, not a lump of sugar. Monique says that Renata did not do any baking on the day she disappeared. This upsets me very much because I would like to feel that she is keeping herself alive on her miserable little cakes.

I have informed the police that she is missing, and have had her description circulated in all the precincts. A police officer came around with a couple of police experts, who took a few over-quick, over-cursory fingerprints from things that Renata had to have touched in her room. The police officer then got rid of the experts and he asked me to make him some coffee and he settled himself down in my kitchen as if he had all the time in the world and all he wanted to do with it was to sit around and chaff and gossip and relax.

The police officer was one of those big, clumsy, bull-like men who move around very slowly and have tired little I-have-seen-it-all eyes. He had a scarlet neck which looked as if it had absorbed more experience than his face, and it came bulging over the collar of his uniform with every inch of its weatherbeaten surface decorated by the most unpleasantly elaborate lithography of deep cracks and creases, which were all overlaid by a feathery tissue of spider-web lines.

He asked me if I knew how many young girls disappear in Manhattan every year and are never heard of again. I managed to change the subject, so that he never got the satisfaction of telling me. I knew the figures had to be extremely alarming just from seeing the amused cynical expression on his face when he asked me the question.

Almost immediately I started to take an immense dislike to him. I hated the way he lit a cigarette and leaned back in his chair smoking it very slowly. I hated the way that when I had made him coffee, he sipped it much too slowly.

'This is a pretty nice place you have got yourself here,' he said as he examined my kitchen with a connoisseur's worldly-wise eye. He made it only too plain that he had very little interest in asking me any questions about Renata. Her case obviously bored him, and he seemed to have already given it up as hopeless. I found it both irritating and ironic to realise that for the moment all that really interested the police officer was my apartment.

He asked me if he could take a look at the front room, and when he saw it he behaved exactly as I feared that he was going to behave. He became intolerably over-excited and overwhelmed by my beautiful view.

'This is out of this world! This sure is out of this world!' he kept repeating, as he went slowly ambling round the room and gazed out through the plate glass windows in a fatuous state of rapture.

'You've certainly got a lot going for yourself up here!' he said, and he whistled through his chipped black teeth to show his admiration, and every crack and crease in his scarlet neck seemed to open up, as if they too were exhaling his approval. I'm afraid that of all the people who have visited my apartment no one has ever seemed to really love it quite as much as the police officer.

He wanted to know exactly how many bedrooms there were, how many bathrooms. He wanted to know if the building had a porter, how was the apartment heated, how much did I pay for my rugs, did I ever have any noise problems from the people who lived below?

'I guess your maintenance costs must be pretty high. But I know that if I had a really sensational place like this, I would figure it was worth it!'

I felt I might start to scream if he went on like this, for he seemed to have completely forgotten he was meant to be working on a case. I had the awful feeling that in his mind this wretched man had already moved me out, that he was now starting to move in his wife and his furniture and his police-officer kids, and he wanted nothing to distract him from his pleasant fantasy that he was going to live, happily ever after, with them all in my apartment.

'This place has real class,' he said. 'You feel it the moment you walk through the door.'

I interrupted him quite rudely and asked him if he thought there was any hope that Renata would ever be traced.

He gave a lazy cynical laugh. 'New York is a very big city!'

I asked him if he wanted to take down the details of the girl's disappearance. He got out a note-pad with an air of bored and weary condescension, as if he was only going through a pointless police ritual to please me. He asked me how long the girl had been missing. I found this utterly infuriating, for I had already told him innumerable times and I felt that he should have been able to remember the answer if he had not been so drunk with his passion for my apartment.

When he grasped that she had been gone for three days he gave one of his lethargic and worldly sighs. 'Missing for three whole days and not a word from her . . . Oh boy! That doesn't sound so good. This city is crazy, lady! This whole city is insane!'

The police officer then asked me if I knew anywhere that Renata was likely to go to. Did she have any close friends in the city? Did she have any relatives? Did she have a boy-friend? I found it quite difficult to explain a person like Renata to this bored and bull-like officer. I had to tell him she was not someone who made friends very easily, that apart from her father I could not imagine who she could go to. He asked me if the girl had seemed to have anything on her mind on the day that she vanished. Did she have any problems? I told him that if she had any special problems I couldn't imagine what they could be. I only longed for him to go. It seemed pointless to keep on talking to this man who only really wanted to know about the maintenance costs of my apartment.

'Well, I guess that's it,' the police officer said. He seemed quite sorry to go, as if he hated to tear himself away from my spectacular view. 'An apartment like this must make you feel on top of the world!' Those were the last words that this slow-moving monster said, as he took his horrible, corrugated neck out through my door.

Yours in a state of impotent,
almost inexpressible, anger,

J.

Dearest . . .

A few hours ago I sent a cable to Arnold's Paris hotel asking him if he has heard from Renata. He has cabled back the word 'no' with nothing else added. I loathe Arnold. He really is a heartless son of a bitch.

I don't think that Renata even knows Arnold's address. Even if she does know his telephone number, I can't imagine that someone as ignorant and inept as that girl would be capable of placing a long-distance call. Even if she knew how to contact Arnold, I have the idea that she would never dream of doing it. If she was starving, I am afraid that she would think it was wrong to bother him after he had been so 'great' to her. No doubt that poor muddled creature would persuade herself that her beloved mother would think it would be wrong.

As the hours go by—and still no word from her—I find that I am getting more and more distraught. I have a horrible suspicion that she has not even got a dollar on her.

I used to buy her little things if she asked for them, but I never gave her any money of her own.

What will become of that girl, alone in the city without even the money to buy herself a cup of coffee? For the last few days the temperature has been ten above zero. I find myself frantically turning on the TV to listen to the various weather reports, for I keep praying they will predict the weather is going to improve. An hour ago I felt like throwing something at the glass of the TV set when the weather man kept blandly smiling as he announced that tonight they expect a much more severe, much colder spell.

Sitting here in the warmth of my central heating, the weather looks quite pleasant when I look out of my window. The winter sky looks very pure and pretty, with little streaks of palest green, palest mauve, palest yellow, all the delicious colours of Italian ice-creams. But this morning I went down in my elevator and took a little walk in the streets. I was horrified to find that one of those really cruel icy winds was blowing. It was one of those winds that blows its freezing air into your lungs with such a force it can prevent you from getting your breath. I only stayed out for a very short time and I was very warmly dressed with wool-lined boots, a fur coat and a Russian snow hat, but when I came back inside I had to take a hot bath, my whole body was so stiff and frozen and blue.

Where can Renata have been sleeping for the last three nights? I can only hope to Christ that she has been lying like some derelict bum on top of those stinking vents which let up warm steam from the subways. I have been wickedly lazy about getting her good clothes for the winter. A month ago I noticed that her snow boots were worn through, that she badly needed a heavy full-length coat to replace that short woolly jacket which is all she has to wear. I was always intending to take her out shopping. Somehow I never got around to it.

How will she avoid getting pneumonia or frost-bite if she is sleeping out on the side-walks in this gruelling Arctic weather? I am not even certain that she owns a pair of warm gloves. I asked Monique, but she said she couldn't remember.

I keep trying to imagine what I would do if I found myself in Renata's desperate position. I suddenly wondered if she could be trying to head for Los Angeles in the pathetic hope of finding her mother.

I have swallowed my pride and I have once again cabled Arnold asking him to send me the address of Renata's mother's hospital. I very much doubt that he will trouble to answer me. Arnold must have many important things to occupy him in Paris, and I would suspect that Arnold will now choose to regard Renata's fate as entirely my affair.

I only pray that Renata is not already on her way to California crazily hoping to find her mother. I hate to think of that friendless girl setting off on such a hopeless quest and trying to walk across a whole continent in the winter alone.

It is very strange. I would never have believed that I would feel so concerned, so desperately upset. If only I could feel more certain that Renata was still alive.

I shiver when I think that for three long nights Renata has been wandering the streets of New York dragging her canvas bag. Already she may have been raped—already she may have been mugged. The only time that aggravating scarlet bull of a police officer showed that he has a single brain in his head was when he said that this whole city is insane.

I find it unbearable to imagine a bunch of vicious drug-crazed thugs jumping out at Renata from some murky doorway. I see them all kicking her and kicking her as she lies there writhing on the sidewalk. I see them cracking her over the head with a broken whisky bottle as they grab her canvas bag. The scene is almost as horribly vivid to me as if I had actually seen it. I have not been able to sleep at all for the last two nights and I find that I am starting to suffer from those hideous eerie hallucinations which can sometimes be induced by insomnia. If I hear a cat wailing in the street, it sounds like a human scream, and my heart starts to pound like an engine that has gone berserk, for I feel convinced I have just heard the scream of Renata.

Whenever I hear an ambulance racing by in the night with a shrieking emergency siren, I have the sickening feeling that if I want to find Renata I should get up and follow it to its destination. If only I was not such a coward, I am quite certain that I should now be making the rounds of every casualty ward, of every hospital in New York City. I despise myself, knowing I shall never have the courage to do it. When I think of Renata now, I can only see her as so lonely and vulnerable that I feel my very sanity would snap if some doctor was to point to something lying under a white sheet and tell me that the girl had been set upon and strangled by some perverted blood-besotted stranger. I would find it so insufferable I hardly feel I could survive it if some nurse was to tell me Renata's poor plump body had been stabbed.

She was always such a timorous creature. She was frightened of cats, and kettles and insects, and Christ knows what else. It must have taken enormous courage for her to force herself to go out through the door of my apartment into nothing. I really prefer not to try to imagine her suicidal state of mind when she came to the decision that disappearing was the best thing she could do.

I was wrong to be so certain that Arnold would never take the trouble to answer my last cable. Lately I have been too wrong about too many things. Arnold's cablegram reads: 'What on earth has happened. Feel desperately alarmed and worried. For God's sake let me be informed immediately.' He also encloses the address of Renata's mother.

I am only now starting to realise that in his peculiar and uneven way Arnold has always taken much more responsibility for Renata than I would have ever expected him to do. Whereas he has been extremely unreliable to me, he has not been nearly so unreliable to her.

When I think back to the past in the light of all the new things I now know, it would seem that in his feelings and behaviour towards Renata, Arnold has always been extremely ambivalent. On occasions he can treat her with a contemptuous and brutal indifference, as if he still blames her and wants to punish her for the unhappy and ugly years which he wasted with her mother. But just when one thinks the girl means nothing to him—he will suddenly show that there is another side. It would appear, from what Renata told me, that Arnold has always showed her much more concern and affection in private than he is ever able to show her in public. When other people were present he always tried to dissociate himself from the girl, for he seems to find it painful when he has to present such an ungainly misfit to the world as his daughter. But although it obviously distresses and embarrasses him when he has to pretend he has a blood tie with the girl, it must still be remembered that he has always refused to do the thing which it might seem easier for him to do. He has never publicly denied that she was his daughter. He lied to me. He lied to everyone else for her sake. Insofar as he has been emotionally capable, Arnold has tried to act as Renata's shield.

I am only now starting to grasp the fact that, in some complicated way, Arnold is oddly fond of Renata. Something in this unloved and down-trodden girl seems to bring out something protective in this man whom I can only see as fiercely unprotective and uncaring. In a sense Renata was quite right to feel that it was 'great' of Arnold to arrange for her to come and live with us. As the girl so aptly said, 'he didn't have to.'

I naturally find the way that Arnold behaved to me over the whole affair was so sly and deceitful as to be unforgivable. But that does not mean that Arnold was not doing what he thought was best for his weird non-daughter. I am only now starting to think that it is very possible that when Arnold made up his mind to leave me he may have given quite a lot of careful thought to the future of Renata. Maybe I even should try to see that he was giving me some kind of a backhanded compliment when he decided that the girl would have more chance of finding a little

stability and happiness if she continued to live on here in
this apartment with me, rather than if she were moved to
France, where she would have the disruptive experience
of being asked to adjust to a new and totally alien way of
life. I still have to feel chilled by the idea that when Arnold
made his plans to abandon me my future was a matter of
complete indifference to him, while the shaky future of
Renata caused him quite a lot of concern.

As I now see it, all Arnold's excessive generosity
towards me has been little more than a bribe. Since he
left me, all he has cared about is that Renata should continue to be provided with a stable, comfortable and hopefully happy home. Now that the girl has disappeared I
am starting to feel weirdly ill-at-ease sitting here in this
over-large, expensive apartment. I feel corrupt, almost
like a usurper. The very walls that surround me no longer
seem to be mine when I remind myself that when Arnold
made an enormous financial sacrifice in order to provide
me with all this luxurious, spacious, accommodation, he
was never making it for my sake. He made the sacrifice
only for Renata.

Yours in a state of restless anxiety,

J.

Dear . . .

My door-bell rang a couple of hours ago. I ran to
answer it like a frantic dog that has been waiting for the
return of its owner. I hardly dared to think. I hardly dared
to hope. I rarely pray, but as I rushed to the door I think
I may have actually prayed that when I opened it, there
would be Renata.

My prayer was not answered. In my doorway, instead of the plump awkward figure with a canvas bag that I wanted to see, there was the thin, unwelcome figure of Martha Weller.

'I've come around to see what's going on here,' she said aggressively. Her nose looked very long to me, beak-like and prying.

'Nothing much is going on, Martha. I don't know what you mean.'

'The way you have been acting for the last weeks—it isn't good enough you know.'

'I am not aware that I have been acting in any special way.'

Martha gave a sniff and started to push past me.

'I've got a lot to say to you, but I don't want to say it standing out here in the hall. Aren't you going to ask me in, for Christ's sake? What the hell is the matter with you? You look as if you are planning to slam the door in my face.'

I asked Martha to come in. I still felt so dazed by the disagreeable surprise of seeing her that I found it quite hard to be polite.

When she came in, Martha just stood there in the front room of my apartment and stared at me.

'It's as bad as I thought,' she said. 'You look perfectly ghastly.'

Martha came over and took hold of my face in both hands, a habit I have always found over-intimate and unpleasant. I felt that her bright inquisitive yellow hazel eyes were trying to photograph every fault and wrinkle in my skin.

'Jesus!' Martha gave a long whistling sigh. 'I can see now that I was certainly right to come here.'

'I'm perfectly all right, Martha,' I said irritably. 'Let me get you some coffee.' I wanted this woman to let go of my face.

Martha followed me into the kitchen. She hovered around behind me, scrutinising every movement that I made. While I was pouring out the boiling water from the kettle, my hand shook, and Martha noticed.

'We've certainly got to do something about you,' she said. 'I guess I must be psychic. I somehow knew you were having a crack-up just from the way you've sounded lately when I've got hold of you on the phone.'

'I'm not having a crack-up, Martha.' I wondered if my voice sounded quite as cool and balanced and brusque as I would have liked. 'And frankly I must say that I rather resent the way you seem to have come here in order to make a lot of insulting remarks.'

'You can't hide away from the truth,' she said to me. 'You can get as mad at me as you like. I don't care. I've been too fond of you, for too long, to allow you to fall apart under my very eyes. You just take a look in the mirror— and then you tell me that nothing is wrong. Look at your sinuses for a start. You can't be allowed to go around with your sinuses swollen up like that. They look disgusting. They look disfiguring. A woman's whole looks, her whole sense of herself, depends on well-drained sinuses. I'm going to make you an appointment right away with my doctor. We'll have those passages cauterised by the end of the week.'

'Please, Martha . . .' I said. 'I can tell you at the moment my sinuses are the least of my problems.'

I should never have said this. As I spoke I saw the knowing gleam in Martha's yellow hazel eyes and I realised I had fallen into a trap.

'So you do have problems! Ah now, we are starting to get somewhere at last. You can have your sinuses cauterised every week till kingdom come, but that's only getting at the symptom. If something is bothering you inside yourself, it's an infection. The more you bottle it up—the more it's going to come out somewhere. You've got to learn to open up—to spill everything out to your friends—to stop being so goddam up-tight. If you feel that you have been humiliated, you have got to learn to dare to yell and scream that you feel that way. Women have become paralysed. It's the culture. It's the culture that has made us all lose the courage to be ourselves when we are hurt—to really yell and scream.'

I told Martha Weller that I had not the slightest desire to start to yell and scream. I told her this in the most icy and snubbing way that I could manage. As I spoke, I knew that I was telling a lie. I wondered what Martha would do if I was to take her advice, if I was to suddenly start to yell at her that I really would go crazy if she didn't remove herself and her prying solicitude, so that I could be alone, to think, and breathe, in my apartment.

'I came round here because I wanted to help you,' Martha said. 'But you haven't made me feel welcome from the moment I arrived. I don't seem to be able to say the right thing to you. Everything seems to make you mad.'

Martha suddenly looked both hurt and depressed, and for a moment I felt guilty that I had been so curt and hostile to her.

'I'm sorry,' I said.

'I'd do anything for you,' Martha said. 'You know that.'

'Yes, I know that, Martha. But there isn't much you can do.'

Martha had always been very generous to her friends. I knew that it was true that she wanted to help me, but Martha's kindness was so tarnished by her need to correct, to dominate, and remould, that it seemed quite useless to me.

'If I've seemed distracted and grumpy it's only because I have got a very bad cold,' I told her. I only wanted to throw red herrings to Martha. I hoped to start her off on a new sermon about my sinuses.

She suggested we both go into the front room, and she settled herself down on my sofa.

'Why don't you stop being so grumpy and defensive, honey,' she said. 'Let's relax . . . You tell me everything that has been happening to you. I long to know how it has all come out for you over the whole business of the divorce.'

'It's all been fine. It's all been very amicable. As these things go—I guess it's been everything that one could wish.'

As I spoke I found myself staring with a kind of terror at Martha's thick-soled shoes. I noticed that she was starting to take them off as she sat herself down. Those cast-off bulky shoes seemed like an omen that Martha was planning to spend a very long time in my apartment.

'I have a first-rate lawyer,' she said. 'He handled my divorce from Arthur. I was really very satisfied with everything he did for me . . . ?

'I don't need a lawyer, Martha.'

'Who gets this apartment?'

'I've got this apartment.'

'And what about the settlement?'

'The settlement is more than adequate.'

'And what about the pictures and the furniture?'

'I've got the pictures and furniture.'

'Things could be worse.' Martha settled herself back in my sofa in such a pleased and proprietary way, that it was as if she saw herself as its joint owner.

'Now we must concentrate on just one thing,' she said. 'We have got to try to get your morale back into shape.'

Martha asked me if she could have a Scotch instead of more coffee. She said that she rarely drank in the daytime —that she figured this visit was special. She insinuated she was only drinking because the seriousness of the situation demanded it, like someone who felt they were forced to drink at an Irish wake.

When she drank her whisky the burn of the alcohol made her cough and she made unpleasant sounds in her throat as if she was gargling with disinfectant.

'They tell me his new French girl is a very lovely creature.'

'Do they?' I said.

'Rita happened to see him dining in some little restaurant on the Left Bank when she was over in Paris last month. She said he looked very delighted with himself. Arnold and the girl were sort of flickering together in the candle-light and they were holding hands across a red check table cloth and the whole thing looked very intimate and amorous.'

'Oh did it,' I said.

'When Arnold saw Rita he quickly paid and left. I guess he was embarrassed to meet her eye.'

'I guess he was,' I said.

'Rita says that she has to admit that Arnold was looking very well—somehow much more relaxed and sort of younger than he ever looked with you. His new French girl is only a child, you know. Apparently she's about twenty-three but she looks like a ravishing teenager. The girl looked as if she was just crazy about Arnold. She just kept gazing at him as if she felt he couldn't do wrong. Anyway Arnold looked better than he has for years. I guess he must see this girl like some kind of health cure.'

'I guess he must,' I said.

'But the whole thing won't last,' Martha said. 'So you don't have to lose any sleep over that. Arnold can't have a real relationship with any woman. Arnold doesn't want a relationship. That man only wants a dictatorship.'

'I wouldn't really say that,' I said.

'You couldn't see what he was doing to you, honey. You were always looking at things from the inside. You couldn't see how it looked to your friends who were on the outside. Arnold uses the sandpaper technique. All he seemed to want to do was to sand away all the rough edges of your confidence.'

'I don't think that Arnold ever really had any special interest in doing that,' I said.

Martha then told me that it was obviously too early for me to be able to see my life in any perspective. 'There's only one thing that it is really urgent that you do now,' she went on. 'You must move out of this place tomorrow. You must move into my apartment. I have two good spare rooms, so I can easily take the child and your maid.'

'Why on earth should I move into your apartment?'

Martha's suggestion both startled and appalled me. I couldn't see the slightest reason why Sally Ann, Monique and myself should suddenly have to move into Martha's dark little stuffy place on West 11th Street when the one thing we had was a comfortable and convenient apartment.

'Memories!' Martha said in a portentous voice. She screwed up her eyes, so she suddenly looked like a clair-voyant gypsy who had gone into some kind of mystical trance. 'For you this apartment must be nothing but bad memories. No one can live with that—they can destroy you. Unhappy memories are like a cancer—they eat right into your cells.'

Martha went on to say how much better I'd feel once I moved into her place. She said she would enjoy spoil-ing me—that all I needed was a lot of pampering at the moment. She promised that she would bring me breakfast in bed every morning with freshly squeezed orange juice, proper hand-ground continental coffee and an English muffin.

'There are moments in life when what a woman really needs is a wife,' Martha said smiling, as if she was very pleased with her poem.

I thanked her very much for the offer but said I felt too unsettled to make any move at the moment. I saw a look of anguish and disappointment come into her yellow-green eyes, and it reminded me that despite her officious and confident facade Martha was a woman who had lived alone for many years and had often felt neglected and lonely.

'There are some people who just won't let you help them,' she said.

She started to tell me once again how much she had worried about me, how much Rita and Dodo and all my friends were worrying about me, that I'd always been a beautiful woman but in all the time she had known me she had never seen me look so bad. All the time she was speaking, I hardly listened to her. All the time she needled and flattered, and scolded me, I found that I couldn't stop thinking about Renata.

'Whatever happened to that girl?' she asked.

'What girl?' Martha's question had made me give a guilty little start.

'The half-wit.'

'Which half-wit?'

'That daughter of his.'

'She is in Paris with her father.'

Martha gave a big sigh. She told me that I ought to be grateful for small blessings. 'I just don't know how you put up with that girl for so long. I never understood how you could stand having a nightmare like that in your house. Just the look of that girl frightened me—I always thought she was really bad news.'

Martha went on to say that she had always thought I was a saint to let Arnold impose Renata on me—that she had always felt my whole character was much too passive.

'Martha,' I interrupted. 'I don't mean to be rude, but I really have to go out right this minute.'

'Where do you have to go to?'

'I have a date for lunch.'

'Who do you have a date with?'

'No one you know.'

'Someone new?' Martha asked me coyly.

'Yes,' I said irritably. 'Someone new.'

'You shouldn't let someone new see you with your sinuses inflamed like that.'

'That's a risk I'll have to take.'

'I guess it's your life.'

'Yes. It's my life.' I snapped at her as I went to get my coat. Once I had finally managed to make Martha leave my apartment I walked the streets for some time before I crept back home.

Yrs. in a state of total exasperation.

J.

Dearest . . .

Ever since Martha left, I have been trying to write to Arnold. I know that I now have to tell him the ghastly thing that has happened.

My peculiar second cable asking for the address of Renata's mother has obviously upset him very much, and he seems to guess at last that something is seriously wrong. I would prefer to put through a long distance call to Arnold, to speak to him rather than write to him, but I have far too great a horror that his French girl might answer the telephone. I keep starting to write letters to Arnold, but I find that I always abandon them in the middle. Letters that are written only in the head present far fewer problems. When I try to write to Arnold, I can't think of the right words to describe what has happened to Renata—the facts look far too bald and bleak when I see them scribbled on a page. When I put off writing to Arnold I am playing for time. I am still always hoping that Renata will suddenly come home, that she will suddenly be found, that I will never have to tell Arnold what I have done to this girl whom he left in my care.

I am now suddenly convinced that if I was to let Arnold know that Renata has vanished, that she may well be in danger, he would be quite prepared to leave his French fiancée and would fly tonight to New York. There is absolutely no point in my asking him to come. There is no possible way he could trace her. Our only hope now is the police, and yesterday that preposterous police officer telephoned me to say that unless Renata commits a felony he sees very little chance that they will ever pick her up.

At this terrible anxious time, it is in some ways a relief to understand at last that Arnold has always been much more concerned about Renata's welfare than I ever chose to believe. I still find it a little sad and shattering to realise that this man whom I lived with for so long would be quite prepared to fly the Atlantic at a second's notice if he felt he could be of any help to Renata—whereas I very much doubt that Arnold would take the trouble to come to see me if he knew that I was dying in the very next block.

Ever since my conversation with the girl, I find it much easier to understand why Arnold feels this surprising loyalty towards her. He finds her very burdensome, and he is often very glad not to see her much, but I think I can now see why, in the last resort, he never totally lets her down. Having shared so many of the events and experiences that have made Renata what she is, I think that Arnold must see something gallant in the way that, although life has given her so little, Renata still makes her instant cakes; and she still goes on creating instant fathers from the racing drivers that she sees on the TV—making the very best of the very little that comes.

When Renata told me that she would soon be leaving, I never for a moment believed her. I thought she was being histrionic, that she was only making a wild dramatic statement in order to make me beg her to stay. Now, much too late, I understand that Renata has her own peculiar kind of honour. She must have felt that it was dishonourable to stay on in my apartment once she had told me what she was.

When I found Renata cold and unsympathetic because she made so little effort to establish any kind of affectionate relationship with her half-sister Sally Ann, I had not, of course, realised that Sally Ann was not Renata's half-sister at all. I now feel that Renata may have deliberately tried to stop herself from becoming attached to the child, for she must have always known she would not be able to live with us for very long, and she may well have had a horror of forming any new human relationship which was bound to end only in separation and loss.

Every time the telephone rings, I live in terror thinking it may be the police calling to tell me they have picked up Renata's body. I see her floating face downwards in the freezing waters of the Hudson and the East River. I see her lying, now no more than a piece of red squashed flesh, on the grey cement of one of the avenues, where in her desperation, she has hurled herself under a car.

If only I could hear some good news of her, Dear So and So . . . I have a horrible premonition that I am never going to find out what happened to her. Days will turn into weeks and I shall still hear nothing. Renata will be a name on the police lists for a while. Then eventually her case will be considered hopeless, and Renata will be a name they will cross off. I shall always go on trying to pretend to myself that Renata is fine, that she is happily living somewhere—that by some miracle that proud little overweight and unprotected creature has survived.

It is all such a waste. It need never have happened. Everything seemed so much better. I was just starting to learn to adjust to her. How I loathe the thought of my future, sitting around in my apartment, endlessly hearing no news—endlessly asking myself the same questions. If I had not shown Renata how much I resented and despised her when she first arrived—would that have made much difference? If, at the end, when my whole attitude towards her was slowly starting to change, I had been much warmer, much more persuasive, when I told her I wanted her to go on living in my apartment—would that have made much difference?

If I had sent for Renata's eccentric protector, Arnold, if I had asked him to fly over from Paris to try to convince her that I really meant it when I said that I wanted her to live on here as if she was my daughter—would Arnold have been able to make her believe this?

If I had asked Arnold to tell the girl that he felt certain that her own mother would have wished for her to stay on here with me—might that have swayed her so that everything would have turned out very differently? Renata's mother still has to be only too real to Arnold and her child, although she can naturally never be more than a hideous, unreal fantasy-figure to me. I should still never allow myself to forget that it is the reality of Renata's distressing mother that gives Arnold, and his adopted daughter, their eerie but unbreakable bond.

Would anything I could have done—or not done—have made the very slightest difference? Or were the seeds of Renata's final disappearance sown long before I even met her? Would that plump and lonely girl, who had been made to feel that her whole life was nothing more than an undesirable accident, have in the end always felt she was forced to vanish into the dark as if in some forlorn way she was really searching for herself when she looked in the cold savage streets of New York for the undesirable accident?

Will only write again if I have good news.

Yours miserably,

J.

McNally Editions reissues books that are not widely known but have stood the test of time, that remain as singular and engaging as when they were written. Available in the US wherever books are sold or by subscription from mcnallyeditions.com.